BALATA

Bretwalda

BY PHILIP KETCHUM

The Draft of Eternity

BY VICTOR ROUSSEAU

Four Corners, Volume 1

BY THEODORE ROSCOE

Genius Jones

BY LESTER DENT

Gone North

BY CHARLES ALDEN SELTZER

The Masked Master Mind

BY GEORGE F. WORTS

The Sherlock of Sageland:
The Complete Tales of Sheriff Henry, Volume 1

BY W.C. TUTTLE

The Swordsman of Mars

BY OTIS ADELBERT KLINE

When Tigers Are Hunting: The Complete
Adventures of Cordie, Soldier of Fortune, Volume 1

BY W. WIRT

BALATA

FRED MacISAAC

COVER BY

PAUL STAHR

ALTUS PRESS
2015

EDITED AND DESIGNED BY
Matthew Moring

PUBLISHING HISTORY
"Balata" originally appeared in the December 27, 1930 and January 3, 10, 17, 24, and 31, 1931 issues of *Argosy* magazine (Vol. 217 No. 5–Vol. 218 No. 4). Copyright © 1930, 1931 by The Frank A. Munsey Company. Copyright renewed © 1958 and assigned to Steeger Properties, LLC. All rights reserved.

"About the Author" originally appeared in the February 15, 1930 issue of *Argosy* magazine (Vol. 210 No. 2). Copyright © 1930 by The Frank A. Munsey Company. Copyright renewed © 1957 and assigned to Steeger Properties, LLC. All rights reserved.

THANKS TO
Joel Frieman, Chris Kalb, Everard P. Digges LaTouche, and Gerd Pircher

ISBN
978-1-61827-183-9

Visit *altuspress.com* for more books like this.
Printed in the United States of America.

TABLE OF CONTENTS

CHAPTER I

OFF FOR THE AMAZON

PETER HOLCOMB LEANED on the rail of a steamer which had already traveled five hundred miles up the Amazon. Although in the heart of Brazil he was as well fixed with creature comforts as if in New York.

There had been a glorious voyage down to Pará, Brazil, upon a superb Atlantic liner; he had danced with Louise and others to the music of a good orchestra, and had paced the broad decks under a tropic moon. Except for one thing, he had been a very happy man. He was hopelessly in love with Louise Gorman—and he had promised her brother that she should not fall in love with him.

Apparently she had taken him at her brother's valuation, assumed him to be a pleasant young chap of no ambition or ability. She had danced and walked and talked with him, and had reserved her admiration for the explorer, Felix Dexter.

Naturally enough Pete hated Felix Dexter, the fellow was a cheerful companion, cultured, mature, interesting, aggressive. He was a young man who shared Lester Gorman's love for wild places and difficult trails. He was tanned and rugged and solid-jawed and cold-eyed, and he treated Pete Holcomb, a man his own age, as an inconsequential kid. Pete was afraid that Louise was in love with Felix Dexter, and there didn't seem anything he could do about it. Dexter was an out-of-doors man like Les, and Gorman trusted him and admired him. If Louise accepted

1

Dexter, Les undoubtedly would give his consent. And Louise certainly liked the brute.

Holcomb and Lester Gorman were both Vardon '22, Pete the most brilliant man in the class, Les the stodgiest and least conspicuous.

Yet Holcomb, in business in New York, was a failure after seven years, chiefly, perhaps, because he paid more attention to the affairs of Vardon University than he did to his own. As class secretary, he was efficient; as a salesman, he was hopeless.

When Les Gorman came to New York after seven years in the desert of Nevada, which he had caused to bloom and pay him half a dozen millions of dollars, Pete, at the end of his rope, had persuaded the young millionaire to engage him as his secretary.

Gorman had talked bluntly to Pete upon engaging him. He had not minced matters. He considered Holcomb a light, worthless, but charming boy who had never grown up; and the young millionaire did not propose to have him make love to his beautiful young sister.

"I want Louise to marry a man," said Gorman brutally. "You're a jumping-jack."

"Louise will marry whom she pleases," replied Holcomb angrily. "But I'll do my best to see that she doesn't fall in love with me."

HOLCOMB had expected that Gorman would go into business in New York, but the millionaire had come East with intentions which he kept to himself. Inside of six weeks he had joined Felix Dexter, a South American explorer, in the project of developing a new industry in the Amazon country; and he gave Pete Holcomb the choice of accompanying him into the interior of South America or losing his job.

"You were the best marksman who ever went to Vardon," said Gorman. "Your record as a rifleman hasn't been equaled yet. I never saw a hunter or a cowboy who could equal you with gun or pistol, so you may be useful to us up the Amazon, though

Silently the two natives sprang upon him.

it's one thing to shoot at a target and another to bring down a man or a beast that's doing its best to kill you. Want to go?"

"I certainly don't," replied Pete with equal frankness. "I hate hardships, and I despise snakes and alligators. But I seem to be all washed up in New York. I know I'm soft and I'm probably a coward; but if you are going to drag your sister on this expedition, I fancy I can stand it if she can."

"Don't fool yourself. Louise is an old campaigner, and I'm not dragging her. She insists upon accompanying us. Have you kept up your shooting?"

"Certainly not. There aren't going to be any more wars. However, I guess it will come back to me quickly enough."

"I've warned you. I'll give you two months' wages and leave you in New York. There is no turning back once we've left civilization behind."

"I won't like it," admitted Pete, "but I don't think I'm a quitter."

Pete, to whom geography had always been a bore, had assumed that they would go up the Amazon upon some such craft as ascended the Hudson from New York to Albany. Instead, they had left the Rio de Janeiro liner at Pará and boarded a transatlantic liner which had sailed from London for the thousand-mile journey up the Amazon to Manáos.

He couldn't get it through his head that the Amazon was a river. It was as broad as New York Bay and, at night, with a complete absence of shore lights, the effect was of being in mid-ocean.

A COUPLE, strolling arm in arm along the promenade deck, passed Pete, so absorbed in each other that the man did not recognize him. They were Les Gorman and the Senhorita Rosa da Sousa.

Gorman, a man's man—granite-faced, Pete had called him— was laughing and looking down into the eyes of the Brazilian girl. If he hadn't fallen in love with her already, he seemed well on his way. Pete only hoped Rosa would vamp Gorman into marrying her and setting up housekeeping in some lovely villa in Rio de Janeiro; it would put a stop to this mad enterprise.

The *senhorita* violated Pete's tenets of beauty which required a girl to be tall and blond, like Louise; but he granted that she had everything possible in a five-foot brunette with golden skin and raven hair and great, black, limpid eyes. She was a vivid captivating little creature who reminded him somewhat of a bird of paradise, the feathers of which were her favorite decoration.

Her laugh tinkled like a melody played on a lute. Her mouth, a trifle too small, was blessed with dazzling teeth and her smile was ravishing. Half French and half Portuguese in descent, she combined the vivacity of a Parisienne with the allure of the Iberian. When an exotically beautiful creature like Rosa set out to snare a hulking brute from the Nevada desert, she wasn't likely to fail. Poor Les had no adequate defenses against this sort of girl.

The Da Sousas, father and daughter, had come down from New York with Les and his party. Dom Juan da Sousa had met Dexter during one of his voyages up the Amazon, and Dexter had introduced the devastating daughter to Les and Pete. With unerring instinct she had discerned the master and the man at a glance, cold-shouldered Holcomb, and set herself out to win the millionaire.

The Sousas were rubber planters, and Brazilian rubber, like coffee, was no longer the wealth-producer it used to be. Asiatic rubber could be grown and shipped to European and American markets at a price far below the cost of getting it out of the Amazonian forests to Manáos and the sea.

Dom Juan, despairing of the return of prosperity, had gone with his daughter to New York in hope of selling his rubber lands for any price they would bring, and was returning disconsolate because he found no purchaser. Of course the wealth of Les Gorman had been grossly exaggerated by the New York papers, but a million would buy far more than its American value in the depreciated Brazilian currency.

CHAPTER II

LIVING GOLD

THE MORE PETE heard about conditions in the country back of the Amazon, the less he desired to inspect them personally. The rivers were full of alligators and other ferocious creatures, the trees were the homes of boa constrictors, the forests were infested with natives who shot poison darts from blowpipes, the temperature was always a hundred in the shade, the humidity was worse than the temperature, and there was no excuse for anybody's going there if he didn't have to.

Pete Holcomb had never felt the love of adventure. He liked soft beds and tiled bathrooms, theaters, films, dances, pretty women in Paris frocks, well-lighted streets, and comfortable motor cars.

It was in a very blue mood that Pete leaned by the rail and looked at the black waters of the Amazon. All the "balata" in the world wasn't worth getting killed by a poisoned arrow in one or having a leg bitten off by a cayman, the Amazonian alligator.

Balata. Pete had never heard the word until recently. It was a white gum exuded by a rare tree commonly known as the bully-tree. It would only grow in the Amazonian country and could not be transplanted to Malaysia as rubber trees had been. There was no fear of Asiatic competition in balata.

Very small quantities of the stuff had been discovered up to date. It was an improvement upon gutta-percha and, if found in sufficient quantity, would drive that commodity off the market. Mixed with rubber, balata had a non-slip quality invaluable in electrical industries and particularly in the manufacture of belts for dynamos.

Since the decline of the Brazilian rubber industry, all the traders were ardently seeking balata, which brought a very high price, and rumor said that the Amazonian woods were full of balata hunters who were murdering one another for the precious stuff. They called it "White Gold."

In a journey from the coast of Colombia to the Rio Negro in Brazil, Felix Dexter had come into an unexplored region containing several hundred square miles of bully-trees, and it was in Colombia, across the border from Brazil. Unaware of the presence of balata within their borders, the Colombian government had leased an area as large as a New England State to the explorer, and he had returned to New York for capital to develop his proposition.

The balata was there, all right. He had convinced Les Gorman of that. But it would have to be taken out across Brazil to the Amazon city of Manáos, through a country where there was less law than in the early days in the American West, where man and nature combined to present insuperable obstacles.

In place of the red Indians. the Amazon forests were infested with diminutive but virulent natives whose arrows were poisoned, and there were ferocious animals, disease-bearing insects, floods, swamps, and every grim hindrance imaginable.

Les, Pete realized, had gone into the thing for the very reason which made the proposition unattractive to him. Gorman liked to tackle hard problems. He got a thrill out of a test of strength between himself and Nature, and he favored the idea of hunting jaguars and shooting alligators and wrestling with snakes and dodging poisoned darts from blow-guns. The man was a splendid idiot. More power to the bright eyes of Rosa da Sousa!

"The world needs balata," he had told Pete. "Well, we'll find a way to get the stuff out. I'll probably make a lot more money which I don't want, but the job is going to be a lot of fun. It will make a different man of you, Pete. You'll come out hardy and strong and self-reliant and confident, and the next time you tackle a New York business man for a job you'll scare him into giving it to you."

ESPECIAL care had been taken to conceal the purpose of the expedition. Lester Gorman, American millionaire, was ostensibly after big game in the Amazon country, accompanied by several guests, and had no other purpose. Dexter had warned him that the impoverished rubber hunters of Brazil dreamed every night that they had discovered balata and woke up cursing because it was not true.

"Let them suspect that we know where the stuff is to be found," he stated, as they were sailing south, "and we shall be trailed by a multitude which will make the Yukon gold rush a side show. Remember, also, that the Brazilians will bitterly resent the success of American balata hunters, the more so as they are starving to death. You see, twenty or thirty years ago, Brazilian rubber trees were planted in the Straits Settlements," explained Dexter. "They flourished, and because of abundance of cheap labor it comes on the market at a price which has nearly destroyed the rubber industry of Brazil and Peru."

"I understood," said Pete, "that the stuff was gathered by Indians in South America. Surely they didn't pay them much if anything. How can Asiatic labor be cheaper?"

"My dear boy," said Dexter with biting condescension, "contrary to the general impression, the native population of the Amazon country is sparse. Hence the cruelties perpetrated upon the savages which caused international scandal ten or fifteen years ago. Having comparatively few workmen, the planters had to drive them brutally. And after the rubber was gathered, the transportation of it was a long and very expensive process."

"You see, Pete," said Les, "we are really going to perform a great service for Brazil. Here is a section nearly as large as the United States which is almost bankrupt by the disappearance of its greatest industry. We shall substitute balata for rubber down here. At present Great Britain practically controls the rubber business of the world. We'll bring it back where it belongs. Thus America is benefited, Brazil is benefited, and we shall take out a fortune for ourselves."

"I doubt very much, Les," said Dexter, "whether balata can ever be produced in sufficient quantity to replace rubber. The bully-tree is a hardwood and won't grow except in certain places, under certain conditions. It won't flourish in flood country as the rubber tree does."

"It has never been cultivated," replied Les confidently. "We'll see what science can do about that."

"In the meantime, Holcomb," Dexter observed, "let a whisper of our business get out and we shall all have our throats cut. I advised Les to go up the Rio Negro with a powerful force, but he insisted upon a preliminary survey with a very small party. Therefore, not a word of our real business."

"Do they have oysters in the Amazon?" asked Pete, grinning.

"Not that I know of."

"They'll have one when I get there."

CHAPTER III

SHADOWS IN THE NIGHT

PETE, TRUE TO his promise to Les Gorman, had only one dance with Louise on deck that night. Dexter monopolized her the rest of the time, and she bade Pete good night as she took a turn around the deck with the explorer, before turning in for the night.

Pete's eyes followed her mournfully; then he shrugged his shoulders and seated himself in a deck chair. The orchestra, having packed their instruments, departed, and the few passengers who had been sitting in the vicinity disappeared one by one. In a few moments the electric bulbs inside the Chinese lanterns went out and it was dark. Pete sat there while he lighted and consumed a cigarette. He saw the lamps in the smoke room go out and then the deck lights flickered and vanished. There was no moon. A few stars and the lantern on the after mast gave vague, uncertain light.

A man appeared on the opposite side of the deck. Pete recognized the figure of Felix Dexter. He had no desire to converse with his rival and refrained from calling out. Dexter walked to the after rail and leaned on it, looking down upon the main deck where a few steerage passengers were sleeping on the hatch cover.

For the first time Pete became aware that the engines had stopped. The steamer had approached shoal water and a bend in the river and was waiting for a pilot who would guide her for several hours until the danger spots were passed. He saw, far off, a few lights on shore. Evidently there was a village over there.

Dexter still leaned over the rail. Pete wondered whether he had kissed Louise good night. Louise was not casual about such things. If she kissed Dexter it meant that she was in love with him. Well, the fellow might be all right, but he wasn't good enough for Louise. He was an adventurer, hard as nails, not likely to appreciate a wonderful woman. If he married her he would hurt her some day. Damn him!

A scraping sound behind him caused Holcomb to look around. He saw a man swing over the rail from the main deck, eight feet below. Another followed him. They moved noiselessly now, barefooted. They were creeping across the deck. The figure of Felix Dexter was dimly outlined.

Fascinated, Holcomb watched the barefooted men glide toward Dexter. That he was their objective did not occur to Pete until the pair were upon him. Pete Holcomb, until the present moment, knew violence only in the columns of the newspapers.

The men were behind Dexter, their approach unheard by him. Silently they sprang upon him. He saw a second's struggle and then the body of Dexter went limp. They were dragging him toward the port rail.

And then the former cheer-leader came to life. Pete was out of his chair and halfway across the deck in a bound. Dexter apparently had been stunned by a blow and the pair were dragging him by the shoulders. Pete was upon them in a second, but they heard him coming and, dropping their burden, faced him.

Crash! He catapulted into one of them, aware, too late, that the man had a knife in his hand. Fortunately the shock of the collision sent the knife flying and dropped its owner, a small, frail fellow, to the deck. The other man crouched and sprang at Pete, who whirled from his first victim and let swing a wild but furious right.

He missed, he heard a swish, and felt a sharp pain in his

shoulder. Realizing that he had been stabbed, he kicked furiously out with his right foot and caught the knife-wielder in the groin. The fellow staggered back, snarled, and was preparing to close in again, when Dexter clambered to his feet and fumbled for the gun in his hip pocket.

Immediately the man with the knife leaped for the rail four feet distant, caught a rope which was hanging there, and slid down it. Pete turned toward his first antagonist, but that worthy was already vanishing over the rail to the main deck.

Dexter, a little groggy, leaned over the rail, and so did Pete. They saw the fellow run to the port side and go over. Dexter's gun was out; he aimed it, then thought better of it and did not fire. Instead he ran to the port rail, and Pete followed him.

There was a small boat alongside which was casting off, and two men in it were drawing out of the water the fellow who had gone overboard.

"Fire!" exclaimed Holcomb. "There they go in that rowboat. You can disable them."

"No," replied Dexter. "Let them go. That's the best way."

The men in the boat had oars out and they slid away into the black night. Holcomb and Dexter watched them until they vanished a score of yards away from the ship.

"**HOLCOMB,**" said Dexter gravely, "I owe you a lot. If you hadn't come up, I expect they would have got me. I never heard a sound until I received a crack on the back of the head."

"Why didn't you shoot just now?" demanded Pete. "If you give the alarm now, the ship's crew can catch them."

"Let them go."

"But they tried to kill you," Pete protested.

"I don't think so. Their game was to knock me out and drop me into that boat."

"But why, for heaven's sake?"

"Well," said Dexter, "I expect they figured that if they could get me ashore they could squeeze out of me the location of my balata concession."

"Oh, that was it!"

"If I fired and alarmed the ship, the officers would want to know why I was attacked, and others on board might jump to the conclusion that it was balata business. Much better to let them get away. They failed in their attempt, thanks to you. How did you happen to be around?"

"I've been sitting in one of the deck chairs over there. I was in the shadow and they didn't see me."

Dexter thrust out his hand. "I'm tremendously grateful. I expect I might have been tortured if they got me ashore. Holcomb, you're one hundred per cent. If the time ever comes when I can do anything for you—"

"You can," said Pete shortly. "Right now."

"What?"

"Use your influence with Les to leave Louise behind. We have no business dragging her into this mess. This is a sample, I suppose, of what we have to expect."

"My dear boy, I've requested Les to leave the girl in Manáos. I wanted him to leave her in New York. I have explained to her that she will be a handicap to our expedition and that her life may be in danger. But it's absolutely no use."

"But after this?"

"I'll go at Gorman again. I supposed that nobody in Brazil knew my business. I secured the concession through Bogotá. But some one must suspect that I found balata. They suspect everybody up there. They are demented on the subject."

"They seem to have particular reasons for suspecting you," said Holcomb grimly.

"Right. Well, we'll have to take extra precautions. I believe you are going to turn out to be a valuable man, Holcomb."

"Thanks," said Pete curtly. "Don't you think we had better go to bed now?"

"Good idea. I won't forget this."

They parted at the companion entrance, and Pete sought his cabin. In the excitement he had completely forgotten the sharp pain in his shoulder, but he remembered it when he discovered that his shirt was soaked with blood. He rang for a night watchman and asked him to summon the ship's doctor.

There was a four-inch gash in the left shoulder, fortunately not deep. Pete told the doctor that he had been set upon by a couple of robbers who afterward jumped into a boat which was lying alongside.

CHAPTER IV

THE DYING CITY

ASIDE FROM A stiff and aching shoulder, Holcomb suffered no ill effects from his wound, which healed quickly. Dexter made no effort to minimize his presence of mind and courage, and Les, for the first time since college, dropped his exasperatingly patronizing and slightly amused manner. Louise, of course, was sweetly concerned and made a fuss over the wounded warrior. However, she could not be budged from her determination to accompany the expedition.

"Where Les goes, I go," she asserted. "Do you suppose I'm going to spend six months in a miserable black-and-tan town like Manáos while you boys are having marvelous adventures in the jungle?"

"You must forbid her to go, Les."

Gorman laughed fondly. "Lou is as strong as a man, healthy as an ox, has the endurance of the devil, and she will stand it better than you or I. I don't anticipate any danger from the rats who tried to kidnap Felix. We are all good shots, we'll have plenty of ammunition, the best arms that money can buy and we'll take a half dozen good men with us. If Lou would consent to go back to New York, I'd be satisfied; but I agree with her that she is safer with us than she would be alone in any Latin city."

During the day the voyage up the Amazon was a never-ending wonder to Louise, Les and Holcomb. The steamer often ran within a short distance of the bank and they admired a tropic forest of supreme luxuriance.

Pete asked the captain why they were not bothered more by mosquitoes.

"Mosquitoes live on blood of men or animals," replied the British skipper. "How the deuce are they to exist in a country where there are no animals and almost no humans?"

"But I thought the jungle teemed with jaguars and tapirs and all kinds of savage beasts."

"Farthur up, Mr. Holcomb. This whole country is inundated about six months in the year. There is a fifty-foot rise and fall of water, and at its height the river is a hundred miles wide. There are nothing but amphibians along these shores, and villages exist only at occasional high spots. However, you'll find plenty of mosquitoes at Manáos if you are looking for them."

They came in sight of that great city of the interior Amazon in the early morning, and the Americans marveled at its magnificence, an inland seaport located one thousand miles from anywhere. The steamer approached a great system of floating docks which the captain said were erected fifteen years ago at a cost of forty million dollars.

"It was a great port in those days," he declared. "A rich wild city, full of millionaires and beautiful women. But now—keep your hands on your pocket-books as you walk the streets, and keep out of drinking places. There are hundreds of men in town who would kill a man for a *milreis*—half an American dollar."

THE ARRIVAL of the steamer seemed as important an event in Manáos as the passage of a through train in a lonely hamlet. Thousands of people thronged down to the quay and a multitude of nearly naked black, brown and yellow men were quarreling loudly for the privilege of helping to unload her.

The passengers said good-by to the officers and moved down the gangplank, where they were almost torn apart by a mob of drivers of broken-down automobiles and carriages drawn by miserable horses.

They drove through a district of substantial-looking buildings and observed that about half the shops and warehouses were closed and in more or less disrepair. They turned into a wide avenue with tram-car tracks, past rows of one and two story shop buildings, two-thirds of which seemed to be padlocked, past elaborate residences run to seed, and finally crossed the inevitable plaza with its rows of palm trees and its band stand, to draw up before the Central Hotel, a building which was impressive, but decadent.

A multitude of porters and bellboys descended upon them and divided up the luggage, a man to each parcel, no matter how small. The lobby was large and empty, but the clerk wore a frock coat and a stiff collar, despite the heat. He delightedly assigned them to rooms. Louise and her brother were given a suite once occupied and especially decorated for the president of Brazil. Its furnishings were elaborate and expensive. Holcomb drew a very large room with a bathroom almost as large, and Dexter was equally well taken care of.

A couple of hours were spent in unpacking, and then a meeting was called in Les's parlor to discuss a card which Gorman held in his hands.

"Who is Dom Carlos Aguedarno?" asked Gorman when the quartet had assembled.

Dexter looked startled. "Has he called?"

"Sent up his card with the statement that he would present himself in an hour to discuss business. A salesman?"

"No." Dexter spoke very soberly. "He used to be the rubber king of Manáos. He is a scoundrel if there ever was one. The tales they tell up and down the river of atrocities committed by his orders would curdle your blood."

"The heck with him," said Les. "I'll leave word to kick him out of the hotel."

"No, no, you can't do that. We shall have to see him."

"Why?" demanded Louise. "I think Les is right."

"You've got to be courteous to these people. They set up to

be gentlemen and they are very sensitive about slights. Men have been murdered for forgetting to return a 'good day.' This man's word travels far up the Amazon, and we don't want to have trouble with him if we can avoid it."

"What's the harm in being polite to this egg?" put in Holcomb, "We're a long way from home, Les, and we'll have enough enemies without going out of our way to create them. Maybe he is the president of the Chamber of Commerce and wants to present us with the key to the city."

"After all, I'd like to see what a rubber king looks like," said Louise. "By all means let's have him up."

"Well, it's a nuisance, but we'll receive him," Les agreed. "Pete, I'm turning your services over to Felix for a few days. He speaks the language and knows exactly what we need here in the way of equipment and you can help him in a clerical way."

"Sure," said Pete. "Though I could never add up a column of figures correctly, and there was always an argument between my bank and me as to how much I was overdrawn."

"We'll get along all right," declared Dexrer. "We'll all lunch here, I suppose?

"If you don't mind, I am going to lunch with the Da Sousas," said Les, coloring with embarrassment. "You three can get along without me, can't you?"

"I suppose we must," said Louise tartly. "I hoped we had seen the end of those people."

"**DON'T** be jealous, Lou," pleaded Gorman. "After all, I'm going to be interested in some other woman some day."

"You're interested in another woman now," she replied. "You're making a fool of yourself."

"How would you like to mind your own business?" he retorted furiously.

"How would you? You have been minding mine whenever you got the chance."

The pair glared at each other and then Les recovered his temper and laughed.

"Some day *you'll* make a fool of yourself over a man, Lou," he prophesied, "and I'll try not to remind you of this."

"Oh, I suppose Rosa is all right," admitted Lou. "But I should hate to have a Portuguese for a sister-in-law."

"Brazilian, my dear; and you're not in danger of it… Rosa refused me last night, if you want to know."

The statement astonished the three, and Les laughed mirthlessly.

"You mean to say that she turned you down?" gasped Louise. "Oh, Les, I'm sorry! How dare she?"

Her anger, in view of her previously expressed sentiments, caused the rather embarrassed spectators of the quarrel to shout with laughter, and Gorman's stern face relaxed.

"However, I intend to persuade her to change her mind before we leave Manáos," he said.

Further discussion was averted by the announcement of Dom Carlos Aguedarno.

There entered a short, well-groomed man of forty-five. He was slender, wore a monocle in his right eye, a small black brush on his upper lip and a frock coat. He carried in his right hand a tall silk hat. He was perspiring freely in his heavy garments, but he evidently considered this an occasion of ceremony.

His was a harsh if rather a handsome face. He was dark, but there was no evidence that he was of mixed blood. His teeth were very regular and white as milk and his eyes were black and piercing.

"Pardon this intrusion," he said in halting English. "I speak French better than your language and I presume none of you but Senhor Dexter understands Portuguese."

Les eyed him with disfavor. "I speak nothing but English, sir," he replied. "I am Mr. Gorman. This is my friend Mr. Holcomb, and my sister, Miss Gorman. I take it you are acquainted with Mr. Dexter."

Dom Carlos bowed. "We have been introduced, merely. I shall ask you to excuse the English of mine."

"No excuses are necessary," replied Louise. "We understand you perfectly."

He bowed to Louise. "Ah, thank you, *senhorita.*"

His bold eyes ran over the girl and he smirked his approval. Pete felt that she had been affronted by his glance, and he wanted to kick the fellow. Gorman also observed and resented the effect of the lovely blond young woman upon the rubber king.

"We will excuse you, Louise," he suggested. "You won't be interested in a business conversation. I assume the gentleman is here on business."

"In a way," admitted the dom. "First, I bid you welcome to Manáos—alas, not so prosperous as of yore, but still a wonderful city. I trust, *senhorita,* that your stay here will be joyful."

Louise bowed, rose and left the room. The light went out of the eyes of the Brazilian.

"Now, sir, what can I do for you?" demanded Gorman sharply.

The Brazilian seated himself, crossed his legs, drew a case of cigars from his pocket and offered to each of the trio, who all refused. He drew one out and lighted it.

CHAPTER V

THE RUBBER TYRANT

"**YOU, SIR,**" **AGUEDARNO** observed, "are a business man. I also am a business man. You Yankees go right to the point; so do I. You are rich, *senhor*. I am not poor. You invade my country. I bid you welcome. I offer to coöperate with you in taking out its hidden wealth."

"I don't quite get you, sir," replied Gorman stiffly.

"Once we Amazonians were rich," declared the *senhor*. "We spent our money freely. We permitted the North Americans to come and share in our prosperity. No longer is rubber a profitable business. We stagnate here in Manáos. We wait the morrow when all shall be happy as before."

"I'm still up a tree," said Les. "I mean I don't know what you are talking about."

"The Senhor Dexter knows, do you not?"

"I am afraid I do not, *senhor.*"

"I, then, speak plainly. In our great forests we have one treasure left, the balata. It commands a price which makes it very profitable to market. It will restore the prosperity to Manáos. We must get it out, *senhores.*"

"Is that so? Go ahead," commented Les with a poker face.

"Our country is so vast. A thousand miles in every direction from Manáos is jungle. It is yet to be thoroughly explored. We have not found the great forest of balata trees which we know exists—but the Senhor Dexter, he has found it."

"News to me." replied Dexter imperturbably.

21

"So we have the situation. You have the secret, but it will not benefit you without my coöperation," declared Carlos. "Without my aid you cannot get your balata to market. Without your aid I cannot market balata. Therefore, I say, let us combine."

"I have no balata," lied Dexter.

"*Senhor,*" said Carlos with a significant smile. "from me the Amazon keeps no secret. My agents notified me, when you began your journey down the Rio Negro, that you had made the great discovery. When you reached Manáos the news was known to hundreds. Had I not, unfortunately, been ill of the fever, we should have done business before you sailed from this city. Well, we shall do business now."

"My dear sir," said Gorman impressively, "you are very much misinformed. Mr. Dexter is an old school friend of mine. I wished to make a hunting trip in the Amazonian jungle and, happening to encounter my old friend in New York, he told me that the Rio Negro district was interesting."

"What do you expect to hunt, *senhor?*" asked the Brazilian softly.

"Oh, anything we can find."

"You will find nothing near the Rio Negro, except caymans and manatees. No animals live in these jungles because of the inundation."

"We'll hunt those alligators and sea-cows then," replied Gorman. "Mr. Aguedarno, you're wasting your time and ours."

The Brazilian rose and his upper lip curled in a sneer. "You assume that we are poor backwoodsmen here, that we have no contact with the outside world," he declared. "I have cables from New York. I know that Senhor Dexter tried to interest three people in his balata discovery and finally made a deal with Senhor Lester Gorman, the great engineer from Nevada. *Now* shall we discuss business?"

Les stood up to his full height. "We shall not, sir," he thundered. "Our affairs are none of your business and we do not need your coöperation in our little hunting expedition. I wish you good morning."

"*Bien*," replied Aguedarno. "That is your attitude? You defy me!"

"I'm just telling you that you are all wet," said Les contemptuously.

"And you, Senhor Dexter: you know who I am and how many I command. Do you defy me?"

"Certainly not," said Dexter hastily. "I simply deny the statement that I am interested in balata."

"It is war, then."

"Not from any wish of ours," replied Dexter, who was obviously alarmed.

"You may reach your balata region, *senhores*," declared Aguedarno, "but you will never take out a kilogram of it. Better that the trees rot in the soil of Brazil than that the gum be brought out to the profit of pigs of Yankees!"

"That will be all from you!" cried the infuriated Gorman, advancing.

HOLCOMB, who had sat silent during the interview, thrust himself between his employer and the Brazilian. Les was in a fighting mood and Pete realized that to strike this man in his own bailiwick would probably have dire consequences.

"*Senhor*, present our compliments to your wife and all the children," Pete said glibly. "We assure you of our most distinguished consideration and we have enjoyed your visit immensely and we certainly feel badly that you have to go."

The black eyes of Aguedarno lighted appreciatively. "*Senhor*," he replied, "you, at least, are a gentleman. I warn you that if you go up river with these thieves, you will never return with life in your body."

"Thieves!" roared Les. "I'll knock him—"

Pete took the Brazilian's arm and led him toward the door. "You mustn't mind my friend," he chattered. "He thought you called him a bad name and he has a hot temper, but he is the nicest chap in the world when you take him right and he didn't realize that you intended to pay him a compliment, but you have trouble with the English language. That's the door, *senhor*. Good morning. I may say that I have never seen a society man in New York with a snappier frock coat or a shinier silk hat. You must give the address of your tailor."

"But certainly, *senhor*. It is Blake, on Bond Street in London."

Aguedarno was positively good-humored as Pete led him out into the corridor, grabbed his hand and shook it warmly and effusively.

"If I had any balata," Pete finished by saying, "I don't know of any one I would sooner share it with and that goes for my last cigarette and my last crust of frosted lemon pie. Good-by, *senhor*. So glad you called."

He returned to the suite and found two exceedingly sober individuals.

"Always leave them smiling when you say good-by," Pete quoted.

"If you hadn't interfered I would have flattened his pan for him," growled Gorman.

Dexter patted Holcomb on his uninjured shoulder. "Pete, you're immense," he declared. "We were in enough trouble without fisticuffs."

"He threatened to have us murdered," muttered Gorman. "The filthy swine."

"Well," said Pete, "I can get his angle. 'Brazil for the Brazilians.'"

"Our concession happens to be in Colombia," Dexter reminded him. "Unfortunately the stuff must come out through Brazil, and the frontier of the two countries is unexplored and unguarded. Les, send your sister back to New York on the next boat."

"Let's all go back," suggested Pete. "All the balata in South

America isn't worth the lives of three magnificent fellows like us."

"Louise must go back," said Gorman thoughtfully. "You can go, too, if you want to, Pete. It looks as though we were in for serious trouble and I certainly wouldn't ask any man to walk into assassination."

For a second Pete thrilled. The prospect of the long trip to New York with Louise was very tempting; but he was shrewd enough to understand that she would hate and despise him for deserting her brother. And besides—

"I enlisted for the duration of the war, in New York," Pete said stoutly. "I am a cowardly soldier, no doubt, but I'll try to stick along."

"Coward!" exclaimed Dexter. "If any man but you called Pete Holcomb a coward, I'd knock him down. I know whereof I speak."

LES GRASPED his hand. "You're a trump, Pete," he declared. "But you don't go into this expedition as a hired man. You earn twenty-five per cent of whatever I get out of this."

"Twelve and a half per cent," corrected Dexter. "The other twelve and a half comes out of my share. If we win through, you'll be a millionaire, Pete."

Tears welled in Holcomb's eyes. "You are a great pair of lads," he asserted. "I don't have to be taken into the company to go along. I want to go. Dexter, do you suppose our visitor had anything to do with the attack on you down the Amazon?"

Dexter nodded. "Very likely. You see he had agents in New York spying on me, and agents in Pará, no doubt, who planted the two knife-men on the ship and arranged to capture me at the only spot where a boat could come alongside the steamer. Failing in that, he had the impudence to call on us and try to frighten us into taking him in."

"Humph!" commented Pete. "I suppose it wouldn't be a bad idea to take him in. He seems to hold trump cards."

"It would do no good," replied Dexter. "All he wants is an

idea of the location of the bully-trees and then he would trim us out of all our profits, if he didn't murder us out of hand. He is a scoundrel and he'll never change."

"He was a fool to disclose his hand," said Gorman. "If we were left unaware that our purpose was suspected we would have been off guard. Now we'll take care of ourselves. I haven't a doubt in the world that we'll get out the balata in spite of this crook."

"We're babes in the woods," observed Holcomb. "Tough babies, though. It's getting on to time to start for your lunch date, Les."

"Will you fellows persuade Louise to go home?" asked Gorman. "Darn the kid, I can drive her just so far and then she turns mule."

"We'll try," promised Dexter and Holcomb.

"What can this Brazilian do to us, Felix?" asked the new member of the firm when Les had departed.

"Plenty. He can pass the word up river to hamper us in every way. He can stir up the Indians against us, prevent us from replenishing our supplies—"

"Shoot us from ambush?"

"I think he is more likely to spy upon us. His game will be to let us reach our concession on our last legs, and then eliminate us. He wants to know the location of the balata region."

"Since he knows about your doings in New York, it ought to be easy to find out. There must be a record of your concession in the files of the Colombian government in Bogotá."

Dexter laughed. "It's only a thousand miles as the crow flies from here to Bogotá and about eight thousand to New York, but actually Bogotá is very much farther away. Not more than half a dozen people have ever penetrated across country from here to Bogotá and it took them from three to six months. Furthermore, there is no record in Colombia of my transactions. A dummy corporation in New York secured the concession. And it is down as a mahogany timbering concession. No, his only chance of locating it is to trail us; and that, of course, he will do."

"Well," said Pete with a smile which did not come from the heart, "a grand time is going to be enjoyed by all. It certainly is no trip for Louise."

"And I depend upon you to help me to persuade her not to accompany us."

"If you can't move her, I can't," said Pete dismally. "She doesn't take much stock in me."

"Well, let's call her in and see what we can do."

CHAPTER VI

A HEAVY BLOW

THE RESIDENCE OF Dom Juan da Sousa stood in the outskirts of Manáos in the center of a large and luxurious garden. It was a long, low villa of wood with broad porches and balconies, and was painted a faded lavender. Like its owner, it was no longer spick-and-span, but a dozen servants still catered to the wants of the family in a country where a servant was glad to earn a few *milreis* a month—the value of a *milreis* being at best about half a dollar.

The prefix "dom" to the name of a Brazilian gentleman is a hold-over from its days under the Portuguese empire. Once a title of nobility, it is still assumed by men of wealth, particularly by those with landed estates. Dom Juan sat upon his screened-in porch and chatted with his lovely daughter while they waited for their guest.

"And during your long acquaintance with this cowboy," he was saying to her, "he dropped no hint of his real purpose in going up the Rio Negro?"

"No, father."

"You are in love with the man and you forgot to do what you were told to do!" he accused.

Rosa's black eyes flashed. "I was not educated to be a spy, my father. You must pardon my lack of skill."

Sousa rose and paced the terrace. "You understand, Rosa," he said harshly, "that under no circumstances may you wed with this North American."

"I can't see why," she protested pitifully. "He is rich and splendid and a man and I love him."

"He is not of your religion, you who have the blood of Portuguese counts and French marquises in your veins; and besides, I have promised your hand."

"But not with my consent," she replied sullenly.

"Are you a Yankee woman?" he demanded angrily. "Are you tainted with the vicious spirit of the age? As my daughter, you will marry Carlos Aguedarno, the greatest man in Central Brazil."

"I hate him. He makes me think of a snake," she protested.

"He is a gentleman and my good friend. Thanks to him we are still able to live as become the Sousas of Manáos."

"I would prefer to starve," she cried defiantly.

"Rosa, be silent. Look, the carriage of Senhor Gorman stops at our gate. During the voyage I have allowed you license beyond precedent for a well brought up Brazilian young woman, but you understood perfectly my reasons. You were warned against sentiment with this man. If Aguedarno knew that you walked the deck alone with him, he would refuse to marry you."

"Then I shall tell him. Father, lay aside your prejudices. Let me marry Lester. He is rich and he will make you rich."

"We shall be rich without your marrying beneath your station!" shouted the old man. "And I forbid you to tell Carlos of your indiscretions. Rosa, for my sake, I implore you, try to discover at what point he intends to leave the Rio Negro for his hunting. That is all I ask."

"Why, that is not much, after all," she said, moved by her father's appeal. "I shall try to discover that for you."

"Let us know into what part of the country he strikes, and we shall soon find the balata. You have agreed with me that it is unfair that Brazilians starve while rich Yankees grow more rich."

"Lester is not greedy, and I believe that he is simply going on a hunting expedition. Come, father, here he is. We must welcome him."

THEY led Gorman to the broad terrace where a servant met them bearing cocktails. As he sipped his drink Les cast an admiring glance around.

"This is palatial, Senhor da Sousa," he declared. "One would not expect to find such a lovely home a thousand miles in the interior of Brazil."

"My friend, we have descended upon unhappy days. I wish you could have visited us ten years ago when prosperity was at its height. There was a society here as cultured as is to be found in Paris, and all the attractions of a great city. You have perhaps observed our opera house as you drove out. Once it contained a company of celebrated singers who gave splendid performances.

"Now, alas, it is infrequently tenanted even by miserable wandering actors. It is typical of the blight which has fallen upon Manáos."

"Well, the world will come to your doorstep imploring you to sell it rubber or something else and then everything will bloom again," predicted Gorman.

"I fear not," sighed Da Sousa. "Rosa, the man is signaling that lunch is served."

They lunched, to the astonishment of the American, upon gold plate, at a table upon a terrace at the rear. The food was delicious and was accompanied by rare wine. No American millionaire could have served a repast which was more impressive than that furnished by this confessedly impoverished rubber planter in this remote corner of the world. Les decided that his advertised poverty was only comparative—in which he was wrong. The debts of Dom Juan da Sousa far exceeded the value of his gold plate and other exquisite household furnishings. and the day of reckoning was not far distant.

Les met the eyes of Rosa across the table and they were so kind that he was greatly encouraged. Perhaps she had reconsidered her decision of the night before. When her father excused himself for a few moments after cordials were served, he determined to grasp his opportunity.

"Rosa, darling," he pleaded. "I was never in love before and it's killing me. Don't you love me a little? Won't you marry me? I can't give you any more than you have here, but I can give you a lot."

She shook her head. "I like you very much, Lester. I wish things were different. When do you start on your journey?"

"If you like me why not marry me?"

"My friend," she said gently, "your sister does not like you to marry a Brazilian girl. Well, my family would not permit me to marry a North American. We are of the nobility, at least so my father claims. And there is religion—that is a barrier."

"You can practice your own religion, darling."

"You do not understand. It cannot be. But I shall be thinking of you always and in fear for you when you go into the jungle. Where do you leave the River Negro, Lester?"

"I don't know. A couple of hundred miles up, I guess. I'm a tenderfoot out here and I leave all that to Dexter."

"That will be at Santa Isabella," she said thoughtfully.

"We go up there by steamboat, I believe. After that we take to canoes for some distance. It's all a mystery to me."

The return of Dom Juan da Sousa ended their *tête-à-tête*.

"**HOW** about you two coming to dine with us at the hotel tomorrow night?" Gorman invited eagerly.

The old man shook his head. "My friend," he said significantly, "we have enjoyed your company during a long voyage and this is our farewell. I have permitted my daughter much liberty because we were in foreign lands where conventions are not strict. Now we are at home where young ladies who are affianced must not be thrown into contact with attractive young men, especially of alien race and religion."

Poor Gorman felt as though a knife had been thrust into his

vitals. Glancing over the shoulder of the Brazilian he saw the little face of Rosa working with emotion, and tears streaming down her cheeks.

"Is—is this true, Rosa? Are you engaged to be married?"

Da Sousa drew himself up and scorched Les with a look.

"I make all due allowances, *senhor*," he said sharply, "but I cannot permit my word to be questioned."

Les saw Rosa slowly bow her head.

"I—I beg your pardon, sir," Les said slowly. "I had no intention—I wish to thank you for your hospitality and to bid you both good-by."

Rosa turned and ran into the house. Da Sousa escorted Gorman to the gate, where a conveyance was waiting into which the American clambered. He sank pitifully upon the torn cushion. In his twenty-nine years, this was the first heavy blow that Les Gorman had ever received.

Les had no means of knowing the weight of parental authority in Latin countries. He did not dream that a girl could be forced into marriage with a man she did not love.

So he bade his romance good-by with a sigh and determined to forget Rosa da Sousa, the beautiful but perfidious. It was a good thing he was going where he would be up to his neck in difficulties and dangers. He would have something to occupy his mind. As for women, he was finished with them forever, except his sister, of course. She was true blue.

LES RETURNED to the hotel shortly after two o'clock to find Louise, Pete and Felix Dexter seated in the suite. The air was tense and full of portent. Louise's pretty mouth was set in a straight line and her eyes were filled with an angry light.

"Look here!" she exclaimed when her brother entered. "Did you sneak away and put these two hombres up to persuading me to go back to New York?"

"I had an engagement, Lou," he pleaded. "We have discovered

that we are up against a tough gang who are going to fight us tooth and nail, so it's impossible to take you with us."

"You don't tell me," mocked Louise. "Well, I serve notice on you that you won't get rid of me."

"Look here, kid," her brother began, "I'm not going to have you hurt in some filthy hole where there is no chance of helping you. Be reasonable, will you?"

"And suppose *you* get wounded in some filthy hole," she retorted. "Not one of you knows the rudiments of nursing. You'd die, so you would. And how do you suppose I'll feel on a steamer or in New York wondering if you have been mur—murdered?"

She burst into tears, which were too much for Pete, who rose and fled into the bedroom. They were too much for Les, too. He ran to her and tried to take her in his arms, but she pushed him away.

"We are men and we have to take our chances," he expostulated. "We shall take a much stronger party than we planned and we'll get through all right. You don't have to worry."

"Bah!" exclaimed Louise. "You make me ill. You big selfish brute, you!"

The two men exchanged astonished glances.

"Selfish?" protested Felix. "Why, we were only thinking of your welfare."

"I'll take care of my welfare. I'll go home on one condition, Les. That you abandon this expedition and come with me."

"But I can't. I've given my word to Felix."

"I won't hold you to it," said Dexter quickly, and he meant it. "I didn't anticipate this situation."

"Well, I won't turn back."

"I'll throw myself into the river before I'll let you leave me behind!" cried Louise. "I'm going."

"You're not!" exclaimed the brother.

"To be frank, Louise," said Dexter indiscreetly, "I doubt if fifty per cent of our force gets through. And you will hamper us."

"The matter is closed," she said stubbornly. "If you go, I go."

"I'm responsible for getting your brother into this," declared Defter. "I'll call off the whole affair unless you agree to return home."

"I won't let you do that, Felix," said Gorman. "I'm in too far to back out. We can't do anything with Lou when she gets like this, and of course the kid would be in agony if she thought I was in trouble and she wasn't around. She really won't hamper us. She is as husky as a man. I guess we Gormans will have to go through this together as we have gone through other things."

"Oh, Les, you old darling," she cried joyfully and she threw her arms around her brother's neck. "So you will let me go."

He sighed. "There would be nobody to keep an eye on you if we left you behind. We've got to get a party so powerful, Felix, that these scoundrels won't dare attack us."

"There is a limit to the size of an Amazonian expedition, you know," Dexter warned him. "A dozen men besides ourselves and our native boatmen and porters are all we can take."

CHAPTER VII

FIRST BLOOD

THE RAPIDS OF San Gabriel! Fifty miles of wicked water, rushing along at twenty-five miles an hour, dotted with jagged rocks, slithering over shoals; impassable for anything larger than a canoe, and canoes mount it only by being towed by human animals crawling along the river bank. The end of ease and comfort for the Gorman Expedition. And the scene of the loss of the good ship "Louise Gorman"—an appalling example of American extravagance, but not such bad strategy at that.

Three days after their interview with the belligerent Dom Carlos Aguedarno, Gorman, Dexter & Co. sailed up the Rio Negro from Manáos. It had been their intention to proceed several hundred miles farther upon the clumsy and deliberate river steamer to Santa Isabel, the terminus of steam navigation, and at that point collect boats and rowers and porters, as did all other travelers who wished to continue up river.

It was evident, however, that agents of Aguedarno would sail with them upon the river boat and that the rubber brigand would be given plenty of time to organize the country against them. To proceed in the usual way would be to play into the hands of their enemies.

It was Pete Holcomb who solved the difficulty. While prowling along the water front in search of Anglo-Saxon recruits for the expedition, Pete saw, tied up at a pier and marked as for sale, a river yacht, some seventy-five feet long, fifteen feet wide,

The big half-breed lifted his heavy revolver
and fired at the truce-bearers.

flat-bottomed and gasoline driven. Her decks were of cedar, her deck house of mahogany.

Five thousand cash bought a vessel which cost its owner sixty-five thousand dollars six or seven years before. As it happened, he had only sent her up to Manáos to be sold a few months before and she was in condition. Her engines would drive her at a speed of sixteen knots.

Dexter bought her that afternoon and in two days she was loaded and ready to sail. A crew of four men were engaged and the party boarded her and got under way on the morning of the third day.

If Aguedarno was angered by their unexpected speed he did not seem to know what to do about it and the expedition started without hindrance from him.

HUNDREDS of unemployed in Manáos were available for the expedition, but Dexter and Gorman found only seven that they considered halfway trustworthy and they had no means of knowing that several of these were not in the pay of the rubber baron.

Two of them, Lawson and Barnes, were sailors who had deserted from an American yacht, which touched at Manáos three years before, and who had gone inland in search of balata. They were seedy, dissipated, and down and out; but Gorman looked them over and thought that they would come up to scratch in a pinch.

There was an Englishman, Hutton, who said that he had been connected with a rubber plantation in the Putumayo district, had been discharged when hard times came, and had ever since been on his uppers in Manáos. He was a sorry specimen, but he was an Anglo-Saxon. They hired an Irishman, Scanlon; a German, Schultz; and two Brazilians, one of them, curiously enough, the dignified clerk in the Central Hotel.

Of the seven, Pete thought that the Brazilians seemed most reliable. The Irishman had been thrown off a Booth liner for confirmed intoxication. The German, who had been a barber in one of the hotels, claimed to be an excellent cook.

They were informed that they were hired for an exploring and hunting expedition and might be up country from three to five months. They were to receive a hundred and fifty dollars in gold per month; wages which made their mouths water. All professed a knowledge of firearms.

So they traveled up the Rio Negro, the great northern tributary of the Amazon, in all the luxury of a private yacht. Louise and the three friends had private staterooms and the German, upon being placed in the galley, proved to be satisfactory as a cook. The hunters slept in hammocks slung on deck—no hardship in that climate; and, for a week, Amazonian travel lacked nothing in the way of comfort.

On the second day out of Manáos they overtook the river steamer and passed her as though she were not moving. They passed rubber plantations run to seed, whose inhabitants rushed down to the quays and waved to them to visit. They saluted politely but did not slacken speed. The days were pleasant and the nights were delightful. Forward, the men sang songs and played poker for promissory notes; aft, the quartet played bridge and discussed the future.

"We'll be fifteen hundred miles inland when we reach the rapids," said Pete. "Your concession can't be more than three or four hundred miles farther, Felix. It isn't going to be so bad after all."

Dexter laughed. "Enjoy life while you may. There will be many a day after we leave the Louise when we will be lucky if we move forward two or three miles. You haven't the slightest idea what we are up against."

"Oh, let us enjoy the present," pleaded Louise. "Have you any notion why the water of this river is so black? It's like ink."

"Hence the name Rio Negro," replied Dexter. "It's supposed to be colored by submerged roots, but I really don't know."

The peaks of distant hills warned them that they were finally leaving the flat plain of Central Brazil and approaching rough water. For several days they had not sighted a settlement nor observed an Indian canoe, but Dexter was hopeful that their arrival below the rapids would draw natives who could be hired to act as porters.

ONE MORNING they came in sight of broken water, and the native captain of the yacht notified them that he could not proceed more than three or four miles farther. So fast was the current already that the vessel moved upward with difficulty.

They made camp upon an outcropping of rock on the northern shore and the work of unloading began.

Dexter, familiar with the difficulties of the journey, had laid in supplies in New York not to be procured in the Amazonian regions. There were stores of concentrated foods of the type used by Arctic explorers and up-to-date voyagers into remote places, and these he expected to eke out with game and fish as soon as they were in the higher country above the rapids. There were scientific packs to distribute the weight of burdens and to enable a strong man to carry a hundred pounds without too much fatigue.

The eyes of the enlisted men widened as they saw the curious things which came out of the hold of the yacht and which were unloaded upon the shore. Despite every effort to reduce the weight, however, there were three thousand pounds, exclusive of arms and ammunition, which must accompany the party.

Furthermore, there was no evidence that there would be porters. As the luggage accumulated, the hired men began to mutter and finally held a conference. The Englishman from the rubber plantation, Ronald Hutton, finally approached Gorman.

"Begging your pardon, sir. May I ask how you expect to convey this mess of stuff above the rapids?"

"On our backs," replied Les curtly. "Yours and mine and the others."

"Including mine," added Louise.

"Yes? Well, sir, we did not expect to act as porters on this expedition."

"No?" sneered Les. "Then you may have a free passage back on the yacht. You and any others who object to doing a fair share of work. Make up your minds quickly, as we'll start soon."

"If any natives put in an appearance, we shall engage them, of course," put in Dexter. "But we are in a hurry and we shall not wait here for them."

The spokesman retired and there was a conference.

"If they quit," said Les, "we shall have to send half the baggage back; but I don't think they'll quit since they see that we propose to tote our share of the burdens."

The prospect of losing precious wages, as well as the willingness of their employers to carry heavy loads, decided the hirelings. They signified their desire to carry on.

Leaving Pete to stand guard over the baggage piled on the shore lest the crew of the yacht be tempted to load it in their absence and run, the journey was begun at once. Louise carried a pack weighing sixty pounds and declared that she found it light. She wore a man's clothing, of course, the same uniform distributed to the men, thin cotton garments of brown, heavy shoes, and leather puttees to protect the legs against snakebites.

PETE WATCHED the line move slowly along the shore, which at this point was rocky and free from obstructing vegetation. He stared after them until they were out of sight and then sighed regretfully as he gazed at the trim yacht upon which he had been so comfortable.

Pete was neither a wealthy engineer like Les nor an experienced traveler like Dexter, but beneath his mask of ingenuousness he had considerable common sense; and he would have sold his prospective twenty-five per cent of the profits of this enterprise for a guarantee of the safe return of Louise Lester and himself to New York. Dexter didn't bother him, because the explorer ought to know what he was about.

In the opinion of Mr. Holcomb, Les Gorman should have had sufficient confidence in his old friend to go into this business whole hog or keep out of it altogether. Dexter had explained the situation truthfully in New York and had admitted difficulties in bringing his balata to market. Les should have taken his word for it, made his investment and then gone after the stuff openly and in a big way.

Instead, the hard-headed Westerner had made the sort of contract which is common in the United States; that is, he had agreed to finance a preliminary survey and, on finding things exactly as represented, had bound himself to put up as much money as was necessary to work Dexter's concession and transport the balata to Manáos and the sea.

When a business man can step on a railroad train, ride three or four hours and inspect an industrial plant before purchasing it, that sort of thing is all well and good, but this meant six months in prowling through primitive Brazil and Colombia with all attendant perils before they would be ready to begin operations.

After reaching this find of Dexter's, they had to return to Manáos and set about doing what they should have done in the first place. While his conduct made it appear as though Gorman valued his money more than he did his life or that of his sister, Pete knew that the real reason was his friend's love of adventure.

Les was confident that he could win through and by his personal experience be informed whether it was possible to get out thousands of tons of balata, assuming that it was still there or ever had been there, in safety. Gorman did not doubt that Dexter had the latex, but he had no intention of taking on the job until he was satisfied that its transportation would be practical.

Pete would have gone about the business differently; but he knew if he had the necessary capital he wouldn't have jeopardized it in any such speculation anyway. He didn't think they had the slightest chance of evading the agents of Aguedarno for any length of time. They would leave a broad trail behind them; their enemies would be on their heels by the time they reached the concession and they would have to fight their way out.

In the meantime it hurt him to think of Louise staggering along with a heavy pack on her back, though he was lost in admiration of her spirit and her strength.

THE EXPEDITION made about a mile an hour and at the end of three miles deposited their loads, left a man to guard them, and started on the back trail which they covered in two hours. They went aboard the yacht for lunch and ate their last civilized meal.

Les and Dexter tried to induce Louise not to carry a pack on the second trip, but she insisted that she was not tired and that she must help set an example to the untried employees. After an hour's rest, Dexter superintended the loading of the human beasts of burden, reluctantly eliminated several hundred pounds of stuff which could be best spared and had it taken on board the yacht which was then ordered to return to Manáos.

With a farewell toot of its whistle, the yacht started its engines and dropped rapidly down the swift current. Pete stood beside Louise as it turned a bend and vanished from view.

"There goes civilization," said Louise gayly. "Does it make you feel badly, Pete?"

"I feel badly that you are not aboard her," he said candidly. "You are perfectly wonderful, Lou, but you have no business on this trip."

"I'll wager I stand it better than you do, pessimist," she retorted. "I'm thrilled to death. The last chance of getting rid of me has gone."

"Come on, men," shouted Gorman. "In three hours it will be dark and we've got to make camp by then."

Dexter led the procession. Louise followed him with Pete behind to give her a helping hand when necessary, and the wage-earners trailed along after, grumbling to one another, while Les Gorman brought up the rear. Les had nearly a hundred and twenty pounds distributed about his person and carried it with ease.

The way was hard. There was a trail, practically a tow-path at the edge of the river, upon which for hundreds of years the bare feet of natives had padded while they dragged their heavy boats against the increasingly violent current; but it was a rough trail, and sometimes the travelers had to bend double to escape overhanging branches.

"Two-thirds of the way," shouted Dexter encouragingly. "And the going will be better from now on."

Holcomb hoped so. He had never carried anything heavier than a suitcase in his life and, despite his large frame, his muscles were soft. His hundred pounds were pulling him to earth. He could hardly lift a foot and lay it down. The sweat was gushing from every pore and trickling down his back in a most irritating manner. He watched the little feet of Louise just ahead of him and, tired as the girl must be, he observed that her gait was lighter than his own.

On, on, on, on. If he gave out on the first portage, only three miles, Louise would despise him. On, on, on!

A SHOUT from Dexter, who had debouched into the clearing chosen for the camp, galvanized them all.

"Hutton!" he bellowed. "Where the devil are you?"

A few seconds later Louise and Holcomb joined him at the edge of the clearing while the others trooped in, one by one.

There was no sign of the Englishman, Hutton, nor was there evidence of the ten heavy sacks which had been piled upon the ground in the center of the camp site.

"Are you sure this is the place?" asked Pete anxiously.

Dexter did not answer. He was running across the clearing.

"It certainly is," replied Louise. "Oh, Pete, what do you suppose has happened?"

Dexter had moved into the bush a few yards and they saw him stooping over. Pete swung out of his load, dropped it on the ground and ran toward him. He saw that Felix was on his knees beside the body of a man who was lying on his face. As Felix rolled the corpse over, Pete recognized the countenance of Ronald Hutton.

The others crowded around and gazed in horror at their comrade.

Dexter rose and faced Gorman, who was white-faced but calm.

"Murdered, I suppose," said Les quietly.

"Knife in the back. His rifle is gone," replied Dexter.

"Indians?"

Dexter nodded. "Acting under orders, of course. War has begun."

"How could they carry off eleven or twelve hundred pounds of baggage?"

"Oh, there probably were a score of them," replied Dexter. "If these were savages acting on their own, they would have torn open the sacks, taken out what appealed to them and left the rest scattered about. Instead they seem to have shouldered the packs and moved right off. First blow for Aguedarno."

"Maybe they pitched the packs into the river," suggested Holcomb.

"Not a chance. In this country the stuff is too valuable."

"Take off your packs, men," commanded Gorman. "Flop on the ground and rest while you have a chance. Felix, you know this country. What are we going to do?"

"We must recapture our luggage," said Dexter. "The stuff which has been taken includes all our trade goods. We won't get far without it."

"Take care of Louise, Pete," commanded Gorman sharply. "Get her away from here."

Louise, who had borne her burden so cheerfully and stoutly, had turned very pale and was swaying. Pete caught her in his arms and led her away. She sat down within a couple of feet of the foaming river and gazed pitifully at the rushing water.

"We can spare the trade stuff best of all," said Gorman. "Thank heaven, there was little food and no arms and ammunition in that load."

"We can do no business with the natives up river without it," replied Dexter. "Money doesn't mean anything to them. If we want work done we must pay them in kind. There seems to be a sort of trail into the interior, opening back of the body of poor Hutton. A mob of men carrying heavy packs are sure to leave a broad track. Depend upon it, there is a plantation in there somewhere and we can thank its owner for this. Well?"

"Of course," replied Gorman.

"We'll camp here and start at sunrise," said Felix Dexter.

CHAPTER VIII

THE ROBBER BARON

THE RIO NEGRO curves like a snake just above the unlucky spot selected by Felix Dexter for the first camp. Some two miles as the crow flies and seven miles up the river was the residence of Senhor Pao Lolita, who despite his poetic name was a grim and despotic half-breed who had moved into an abandoned plantation house and ruled two-score peaceful natives with bullet and whip.

The house was large and at one time had been richly furnished. There was a grand piano whose strings had long since rusted and which gave out a most disagreeable tone. There were fine carpets partially destroyed by voracious ants, and splendid bedsteads whose mattresses had rotted and whose sheets had long since been torn to shreds.

To Pao Lolita the place was the height of luxury. He lived there on what his Indians could grow in a few acres of cultivated ground and upon what was left of a great store of canned goods.

In two or three days the Gorman expedition, laboriously packing its freight, should stagger into the settlement and would be courteously received by the proprietor who would be overwhelmed to learn of the outrage which had been committed at their first camping spot.

But upon the evening of the murder of Ronald Hutton, Pao Lolita lay in a hammock on the ramshackle veranda of the old house while he inspected the contents of a huge pile of heavy sacks which his three Indian wives were slashing open and strewing upon the floor in front of him. A score of naked savages stood in a semicircle and gazed at the wonders with popping eyes.

Pao Lolita was a gross man with negroid features who, nevertheless, had a luxuriant black beard. His dirty shirt was open in front to display a great hairy chest. He had on a pair of very soiled white trousers and wore no shoes or stockings. Beside him on a table lay a belt which contained a huge Navy revolver. On the floor beneath him was a rawhide whip, emblem of his kingship.

In these days of dire poverty in the Rio Negro territory, the contents of the sacks were treasure trove to Pao Lolita and his small black eyes twinkled with satisfaction as each sack revealed its wealth.

Two five-gallon tins of grain alcohol were finally produced. Pao Lolita knew that diluted alcohol would supply the delights of intoxication and ten gallons would last him a reasonable length of time.

Not for months had he touched a cent of cash, nor did the place produce anything for which the traders would supply him with liquors. For weeks he had been forced to go to bed sober and the strain was affecting his never agreeable disposition.

To-day he had pulled off a wonderful stroke of business. In the first place he had performed a service for a powerful person in Manáos who would reward him suitably; and in the second place he had come into possession of a wealth of trade goods and supplies.

"Pack the stuff in the storeroom, lock the door and bring me the key," he commanded of his three naked squaws. "And if you steal a single article in that lot I'll cut off a finger from the right hand of the thief."

He tore one of the tins of alcohol from the hands of a woman, and carried it into the house.

A GUNSHOT woke Pao Lolita from a sodden slumber at an

unearthly hour next morning. He lifted a liquor-heavy head from his filthy bed and listened. The single shot was followed by a succession of sharp reports whose import was unmistakable.

With an oath the chief rolled out, picked up his six-shooter and staggered out upon the porch. From the jungle path half a dozen naked savages were running. From the native huts women were yelling and men appeared waving spears and ancient guns.

Tomo, commander of the scouting expedition, beat his men to the presence of Pao Lolita.

"The white men are coming!" he squealed. "They have killed Fitho and Lonzo. We cannot stand against them."

"Get the men together," commanded Pao Lolita. "There are only a few of the whites. See, already they plead for quarter!"

Four men in khaki had come out of the jungle path and one of them was waving a white handkerchief.

"Only four," shouted Lolita. "Close in and cut them to pieces!"

He lifted his heavy revolver and aimed at the truce bearer. The distance was about sixty yards. He fired. At the same instant a rifle cracked and Pao Lolita plunged forward on his face. Immediately his followers threw down their arms and ran to the quarters where they cowered in the shadows.

"Much obliged, Pete," said Les Gorman as he replaced his handkerchief in his pocket. "His bullet whizzed close to my ear. You did some nifty shooting."

"First time I ever fired at a living target," replied Pete coolly. "I saw that your white handkerchief didn't mean anything to him."

The four men moved cautiously toward the spot where the chief of the settlement lay dead, a bullet in his heart.

Felix Dexter knelt beside him and examined the body.

"A very bad morning's work," he exclaimed. "This is Pao Lolita, a white man, at least what passes for white in this country. It was one thing to shoot at armed natives in the jungle and another thing to attack a white settlement and kill the commander."

"Damn it, man," retorted Gorman, "I waved a flag of truce and he fired at it. Pete shot him to save my life."

"I understand that, but it puts us in a fix."

"I don't see why. No doubt this is the brute who looted our camp yesterday. We'll search the place and find our property."

"It puts us outside the law," said Dexter. "This fellow is in touch with the rubber people at Manáos. They'll make a big fuss about his death."

"He stole our baggage under orders from Manáos," replied Gorman. "He got what was coming to him. Now what's to be done?"

"I don't know," replied Dexter. "I stopped at this post on the way down, but it's fully ten miles down the river to our camp. I had no notion we were at Lolita's after an hour's tramp through the jungle. The river takes a big bend here and we came directly across country. The Brazilian authorities will be on our trail with warrants for our arrest on a murder charge as soon as they hear of this."

"Humph," muttered Les. "What do you advise?"

"I don't know what to do. We have put ourselves into their hands."

"Well, you are the only one of us who knows the country. It's up to you."

"**LOOK** here," interjected Pete. "Since Aguedarno and his gang want to hang something on us, no amount of explanation will square this. We're hunted men. All right. Let's act like desperados. We need porters. We need boats. We need supplies. We've got to search this place in case our goods are hidden here. Whether we find them or not we're on the black books of the authorities so, say I, let's conscript this gang of natives and put them to work."

"Right," exclaimed Les. "Hear that, Felix? Round up a band

of natives and take them back to our camp. Make them tote our baggage up here. Tell the mob hiding in that big hut over there that they are safe if they do what we tell them. Find somebody to take us through the house. If this Lolita person stole our stuff, some of the servants know where he put it."

"This is very high-handed," protested Dexter.

"Well, we're in Dutch anyway. We'll treat these people well, feed them and pay them, and they will be glad that old Pete shot Pao Lolita."

"Very good," said Dexter. "You stay where you are while I have a palaver with whoever is headman here."

He walked away and Les looked at Pete with a frown. "How could a man explore a country like this and be yellow?" he demanded. "Felix acts as though he had very cold feet."

"He knows what we are up against better than we do," replied Holcomb. "And his feet aren't any colder than mine. I've been scared to death ever since I got off the yacht."

Gorman threw his arm over his secretary's shoulder. "I'm beginning to discount your opinion of yourself, old boy. I had my eye on you when we started out on this expedition and I happened to be looking at you when the savages jumped us. You turned deadly pale and began to pump them full of lead. You're a scrapper, Pete, and don't try to pretend you're not."

"I'll say so," declared Scanlon, the Irishman who was the fourth member of the advance guards. "I never saw a prettier shot than what brought that black fellow down."

"Oh, that's too much!" protested Holcomb, who was pink with embarrassment. "Look. Dexter is getting action."

The inhabitants of the settlement were coming out of their holes and cautiously approaching the conquerors. Dexter was in conference with Tomo and was assuring him that he and his people would find the change in the management of the place to their advantage. In ten minutes an agreement was made and tranquillity was restored.

Dexter returned to his friends.

"Pete," he said, "You and Scanlon will take a party of ten Indians back to the camp. They'll bring up the baggage, Les, the headman Tomo tells me that the late Pao Lolita raided our camp yesterday and carried off our baggage. We'll find it in the house practically intact. It seems that there are several boat builders in the settlement. We'll use the natives to transport our baggage beyond the rapids and then have them build us *monterías* if we find none available up there."

"What the deuce is a *montería?*" asked Pete.

"It's a big boat with a deck house. You've seen a lot of them below the rapids."

"Oh, those."

"There are your porters," said Dexter. "Get under way, Pete."

"And hurry," pleaded Les. "Louise will be frantic with anxiety."

CHAPTER IX

WAR TO THE DEATH

THE STOLEN GOODS, in sorry disorder, were piled up on the porch of the residence of the late Pao Lolita when the main body of the Gorman expedition came up.

Louise uttered an exclamation of astonishment at what appeared to be a beautiful villa in the heart of the wilderness, but as she drew nearer she recognized its shocking disrepair. Les saw her, waved a welcome and went on with his inventory of the recovered treasure. A mob of natives, curious as cats, thronged round the new arrivals and exclaimed in wonder at the tall white woman who wore clothes like men and carried a firestick.

Felix met Louise with outstretched hands and held those of the girl longer than Pete considered decent. For many days Pete had resolutely banished his dislike of the young explorer, but now his old hostility came rushing back upon him. Felix had treated him generously, had welcomed him as a partner instead of an employee of the enterprise, and had made him ashamed of his former attitude. The fellow was absolutely on the level and a hundred per cent. No doubt it was jealousy which caused Pete to remember that Dexter had turned green when a bullet brought down Pao Lolita. Even Les Gorman had remarked that he acted as though he had cold feet. To he sure, Dexter had recovered immediately and jumped in and brought the natives to heel. Still...

"We'll lunch here, and try to travel eight miles by nightfall,"

Dexter informed Louise. "There is a good spot for a camp that distance away. Now that we have plenty of porters we'll make good time and we'll be at the village of San Gabriel the day after tomorrow, thirty-six hours earlier than I dared to hope."

Louise gazed with dismay at the mass of provisions and supplies.

"Our lovely canvas packs!" she mourned. "We'll never be able to get that stuff compactly together again."

"It doesn't matter so much since we have plenty of porters," said Les, "We've recovered almost everything. We'll give the women a few trinkets to make them happy and we'll move on as soon as we can."

Pete drew close to the leader. "What happened to the dead man?" he whispered.

"Buried already. Didn't want Louise to see him. Pete, despite Felix's alarm, I think it was a good thing you shot him. He was hostile and he would have refused us porters even if we did make him disgorge the plunder."

"You know why I shot him. He was aiming at you. I'm not happy about it and I'm afraid Dexter thinks it was unnecessary."

"Well, I believe you saved my life. Don't let it worry you at all."

"Would you mind not telling Louise—that is—"

Gorman laughed. "That you saved my life by quick thinking and quicker shooting? Why, she'll be eternally grateful."

"Take me inside, Pete, and let's look at the house," commanded Louise.

ENTERING a wide doorway from which the double doors had fallen and now stood against the wall, they looked into the living room. The girl exclaimed with astonishment. The walls were covered with tiles of pink and green and blue, most of them cracked. The ceiling had been decorated in white and gold with allegorical figures painted upon it like a palace ceiling in Europe. The designs were spoiled because portions of the plastering had fallen.

At the far corner stood a grand piano, its rosewood panels covered with Watteau-like figures. There were gold chairs with needlepoint upholstery and a divan which might have come from Versailles. These were all in dreadful condition.

Louise rushed to the piano, lifted the cover of the keyboard and struck the keys. A dreadful jangle resounded. The wires had rusted and most of them had broken.

"A palace in this jungle and the jungle has overcome it," she said dolefully. "What a pity."

They entered bedrooms with splendid bedsteads and soggy and rotting mattresses which gave forth a bad smell. They came upon a great refectory where a magnificent buffet and a superb mahogany table alone defied decay.

"It's a tomb," said the girl. "Let's go into the fresh air."

"Imagine the cost of getting all this stuff up river from Manáos, especially past the rapids," suggested Holcomb.

"Manáos! My dear Pete, they don't manufacture such things there. The entire contents of this house were brought from France and Spain. Why, the people who lived here must have been millionaires! Poor things. I wonder what became of them."

Privately Pete thought that they were probably murdered by the black brute he had brought down that morning, and he determined to waste no more regret on the rascal. It was a sacrilege for him to have lived in such a place.

They lunched in the open air on fruit provided by the natives, farina—which to the Amazonians is like spaghetti to the Italians—and some tinned beef and at twelve o'clock were ready to march.

Although it was noonday, they were sheltered from the sun as they moved along the river bank by the tall trees which grew close to the shore. While the weather was hot, the intense humidity of the lower country had lessened.

They had been saved by the luckily discovered yacht from the dreadful journey in *monterías* up from Santa Isabel to the foot of the rapids, and they knew little of the dim-lit country with its canopy of tops of amphibious trees, its camps upon ground just solid enough so that they would only sink in it up to their ankles. They had escaped the region of gigantic snakes and the dangers of ferocious caymans.

Instead they had entered the haunts of the jaguar; and the mosquito and piume fly put in an appearance.

Quite jauntily they set out, with thirty savages to carry the burdens. The path was well defined though rough. It was fairly cool in the forests and the insects were not yet thick enough to be very troublesome.

"We'll be able to get fresh meat, soon," said Dexter. "We are coming into a game country."

THE PARTY moved with due precautions, though at this stage of the journey they ran little danger from savages. Vast as is the Amazon basin, it possesses no powerful and aggressive tribes. The Indians of the flatlands are miserable creatures, cowardly and puny, and numerically few, who might swoop down upon one or two white men and fell them from ambush with their poisoned darts, but who give a wide berth to a large and well armed party.

As they mounted into the more temperate regions they would enter the country of more formidable savages, but even these are split up into small warring bands who are ignorant of one another's tongues and who rarely make alliances. Ten sturdy whites with rifles and plenty of ammunition could burst through the native population, provided they guarded themselves from surprise.

Nature itself presented most of the obstacles. Savage beasts, poisonous reptiles, fever-bearing flies, insects which bored into the legs and laid their eggs under the skin, ferocious ants—and, of course, other civilized white men—were their principal menaces.

The mosquitoes were bothering Pete Holcomb who had a tender skin. Unlike the others he did not tan, but grew more and more pink. As the afternoon waned the insects became more numerous and aggressive; and the whites of the party wrapped a veil of netting around their faces and necks and donned cotton gloves which were uncomfortable, but protected hands and wrists. The mosquitoes kept getting inside Pete's face-covering and made him miserable.

The landscape was no longer horrible as it was in the lower Rio Negro. The river roared and rushed by foaming and churning, a lovely mixture of white and blue. Ahead were lofty mountains. The country was rolling and the vegetation on the opposite bank was very beautiful. Myriads of bright blossoms were growing along the shore with rarely a familiar species among them. For a naturalist the country was a paradise, but Pete Holcomb was no naturalist; he kept thinking of Broadway at Forty-Second Street as the promised land.

They pitched their camp upon a rocky point which was clear of vegetation, cooked their dinner over a roaring camp fire, made a smudge which was effective in driving off the insects, and sat around after dinner in excellent spirits. Last night's camp had been a dismal affair. The murder of the sentinel and the theft of half their stores had steeped them in gloom. Tonight all was well.

The natives had quartered themselves between the whites and the jungle and most of them, after eating, had thrown themselves on the ground and fallen asleep.

For the first time the party was a unit. On the yacht the principals had lived aft, the men forward, and the mettle of each was unknown to the other. Now they sat in a circle and got acquainted.

Les, by nature democratic, chatted easily with the German cook. Louise was learning about the hotel business in Manáos from the former clerk at the Central House, and Pete cottoned to Scanlon whose Irish humor appealed to him.

TOM SCANLON was a native of Cork who had been a soldier, a sailor, and a miner, and had wielded pick and shovel in a ditch. He was without education, but intelligent, and twenty years of knocking around the world had eradicated some of his brogue. He was lean, wiry and strong. He had a dot of a nose, a long upper lip and small droll blue eyes, he was ugly but attractive and he was about forty years old.

"Mr. Holcomb," he remarked, "you and me are sensible men. I'm betting neither of us would come wandering into this cursed country if necessity didn't drive us."

"Right," declared Pete. "I like tall buildings."

"Sure, and I'd swap the whole of Brazil for a kitchen garden on Staten Island with a tidy little girl to kape house for me."

"That's not an extravagant ambition."

"For me it is. Every time I lay one dollar on top of another I remember that it can be exchanged for whisky. Do you know how I come to be in Manáos?"

"It's a queer place for an Irishman."

"Well, I was out of work in New York and I shipped on an Atlantic Transport cattle boat for London. They gave me a few dollars and a free ticket home on the steamer. I got tanked up the day the steamer was to sail and I was blind drunk when I got to the docks. What do I do but go up the wrong gangway and present me ticket? They take it and lead me to a berth that I fell into. When I woke up I was out at sea on a Booth liner bound for Manáos."

"How on earth could that happen?"

Scanlon chuckled. "Why, they was short handed and I blundered aboard. Can you blame them for giving me a cordial reception? Well, I had a few dollars left and I gave it to the steward for whisky. I kept pretty completely pickled during the voyage and the scuts chucked me on the dock at Manáos. If you and Mr. Dexter hadn't come along, sure I would have starved to death by now. Not a crust of bread or a drop of drink would these Brazilians give a man without he paid for it. The way I look at it, I'll get cured of the drink habit and have a thousand dollars in my pocket when we get back to Manáos—that is, if we get back."

"Why shouldn't we get back?" demanded Pete.

"They's damn' few balata hunters that ever does," Scanlon replied gravely. "There's a curse on the stuff, it seems."

"And what makes you think we are after balata?"

"Sure everybody knows that. If you hadn't crossed them by scooting up the river on that fast yacht you'd have a hundred of the beggars on your heels. And some of them will catch us yet."

"Do all the men believe that we are after balata?"

"Of course. For what else would a big party like this be running its nose into this blasted country? It's a dirty shame to take a foine girl like herself with us."

"Miss Gorman insists upon accompanying her brother. She's as good as a man."

"Better! When I saw the darling stepping out with a heavy pack on her back, I says to myself, 'There's a woman for ye.' Others might have wheedled the men into taking them, but not one in a hundred would have packed that load. She'd make a fine farmer's wife, that young lady."

ONE BY ONE they retired to their tents. These were exceedingly ingenious and expensive, constructed of heavy corded silk instead of canvas, and supported by aluminum rods. Each was capable of sheltering two persons, and five of them folded into a pack weighing a hundred pounds. Dexter had purchased them dubiously because he was not sure that they would withstand tropic storms, but their lightness and portability persuaded him to stock them.

Two men stood the first watch, Scanlon and the second Brazilian, Valdo. Louise had a tent to herself. Dexter and Les Gorman occupied one and Pete had agreed to double up with Scanlon whom he considered the cleanest of the bunch of hired men, though that was not saying too much.

The moon retired early. While the stars were brilliant they did not shed much light. The fire died down and the roar of the river chanted the company to sleep.

Secure in the protection of the white men the natives kept no watch. The night was very still. The forest noises were faint and subdued.

The sentinels moved about slowly, pausing now and then to whisper a few words. They carried their guns in the crook of their left arms. Two hours had passed since the outfit had retired and Scanlon decided that it was time to wake Holcomb who would relieve him. He moved toward his tent and from the bush a rifle spoke. Scanlon whirled, saw a flash of fire about fifty yards away and emptied his magazine at the spot.

There was no response from the sharpshooter and the Irishman then became aware that Valdo had dropped and was writhing upon the ground.

Men were pouring out of the tents and the natives were all awake and howling with terror.

"Kape down!" bellowed Scanlon, who had thrown himself on his stomach. "There's a spalpeen in the bushes and he's kilt the dago."

"Don't shoot," commanded Gorman. "Those fool niggers are running into the jungle. You might hit one of them."

OF COURSE there was no more sleep that night. Louise proved her worth by dressing the wound of the Brazilian and doing all that an amateur nurse could do to make him comfortable, but the fellow was hit in the groin and it was impossible to stop the bleeding. He died in an hour.

Lying on their arms the little troop waited for another attack, but it did not come.

"The game is up," said Dexter dismally. "Les, I'm sorry I dragged you into this, but I had no notion of what we would be up against. To-morrow we'll start back to Manáos."

"What? How about your concession?"

"We can make a deal with Aguedarno. We won't get much out of it, but enough, in all probability, to cover our expenses."

"You're willing to let a solitary sniper beat you out of a fortune?" asked the millionaire.

"Not one sniper but scores of them. Don't you see the plan? They will pick off our followers, one by one, steal our supplies, wear us down, until we'll reach the concession in such a weakened state that they can wipe us out with one rush and take possession. You and I won't be killed except by a bad shot, but we are likely to be all alone by the time we arrive at our destination. We have lost two men already, and it's impossible to guard against enemies who lurk in the jungle and know its paths. They can move faster than we and they always will be lurking about our camps."

"If we take the back trail." said Gorman, "I suppose we shall be safe enough."

"Of course."

"What do you think, Pete?" demanded the chief.

"Well," said Holcomb, "Dexter has everything at stake. This balata doesn't mean a thing to you and I'd swap my share just now for a ham and egg sandwich. The common sense thing is to do as Felix suggests; but I vote against it."

"Why?" demanded Louise in a curious tone.

"Because I'm a darned fool, I suppose. I didn't want to go adventuring up the Amazon. I would have backed out in New York except that I knew what you and Les would think of me. I hate hardships. This sleeping on the ground has no appeal for me and I certainly dislike the idea of dying up here. However, I think I prefer to be murdered than to sneak back to Manáos and crawl before that yellow scoundrel Aguedarno, and confess: 'You win.'"

"He wins anyway, I am afraid," said Dexter.

"This is the way I look at it," said Les Gorman. "The monkey in the high hat and frock coat threatened me in Manáos. He is responsible for the murder of two of my men. If I only had myself to consider I would go on in spite of hell and high water. It isn't the first time I've had to deal with sneaking coyotes, I've had my hat shot off my head by a hound in the chaparral in Nevada and I considered it part of the day's work. But I've got Louise to think about—"

"You needn't think about me," said Louise angrily. "I'm going on if I have to go on alone. Do you hear?"

"My dear child," said Dexter, "we must think of you. We can't lead you into certain death."

"Rubbish," she snapped. "Both these casualties are the result of gross carelessness and they are your fault, Felix Dexter. You know the country. You should have made better arrangements. You left one man guarding the supplies. You camp out here in full view and tell the sentinels to walk around as though they were in an army post. If you continue to take no precautions I presume we'll all be shot, but I suppose that you have learned by this time that we must expect to be sniped at and act accordingly."

"Come, come, Louise, you can't blame Felix for what has happened. I was just as much at fault," said Les reprovingly. However, he reached for her hand and squeezed it.

"**I HAVE** traveled all over tropical South America but this is my first experience of a shot in the dark," replied Dexter shortly. "I am inured to all ordinary dangers of exploration, but I confess that I am unwilling to cope with a jungle full of white enemies. In all our interests and particularly that of Miss Gorman, I advise a return to Manáos."

"How far are we from the concession?" asked Les.

"A little more than halfway."

"We'll go on. I'll divide the stores with the men and let them go back if they like. Assuming, of course, that you will guide us."

"Very well," said Dexter quietly. "It was my duty to speak as I did, and it was greatly against my interests. I would like to be rich, but not at the expense of you three good friends. My advice is abandon the expedition. If you disregard it, my conscience is clear."

"Good boy," cried Les heartily. "Shake."

"Me too," demanded Louise. "I predict that we shall have no more losses."

"There is another alternative," said Dexter. "In New York I asked you to accept my assurance that the balata was there, and to move up the river with a complete expedition for getting it out. If you are willing to trust me to that extent now, we can return to Manáos and set about the job openly and in such a big way that Aguedarno and his crowd will be powerless to interfere with us."

"I trust you, Felix, but I don't do business that way," replied Les firmly. "There are two things essential to success in this enterprise. An adequate supply of balata, and a practical method of getting it to market. I know already that we need a steamship service to the rapids and a good road along the river and beyond. We need stations at convenient places and an assured service of supplies. It would cost, at a minimum, a quarter of a million dollars to blast our way up to your concession. Before I go in for anything like that I want to inspect your balata country and survey it. Guesses don't go with me."

"**VERY WELL**," said Dexter sullenly. "You realize, of course, that we shall be trailed to the concession and these jungle brigands will be able to help themselves to the stuff for months before we arrive with a strong enough force to protect it."

Les smiled grimly. "I have discovered that they would bring it out on their backs with every possible obstacle against their getting it through. If the supply is so limited that such pilfering would seriously deplete it, then I don't want anything to do with the project."

"Well," admitted Dexter, "I don't suppose they could steal more than a few hundred thousand dollars' worth. I don't think that would deplete it much."

"You *think!* Old man, I want to *know*, and I'm going to find out if Aguedarno had fifty times as many assassins hidden in the jungle."

"That's the kind of brother I have," declared Louise proudly. "Isn't he wonderful, Pete?"

"What I call a twenty minute egg," replied Pete. "I haven't any such elegant reasons for going-on. I'm just gifted with a nasty disposition."

"Then we go on. We four, if nobody will join us," said Dexter.

"Oh, Scanlon will join us," said Pete cheerfully. "He is counting on six months in the jungle to cure him of the liquor habit. He will be terribly disappointed if we go back."

Everybody laughed and the tension was relieved.

Pete Holcomb, in his heart, had hoped that the trip would be abandoned. The way he looked at it, Dexter knew the region, and if he had cold feet, he had ample reason. Pete had voted to go on partly because Les Gorman had so evidently expected him weakly to chime in with Dexter, and partly because, even if he were to be shot down by the sniper within ten minutes, he wouldn't agree to quit in the presence of Louise Gorman.

An expert marksman himself, Pete knew that it was a simple matter for a dead shot to hang on the heels of the party and pick them off, one by one, without much risk to himself. If there were a number of snipers the company would be exterminated so much sooner. He believed that he was voting for his own execution when he took his stand, but he hoped to be outvoted.

But the New Yorker did not know that there were very few skilled marksmen in the jungles of the Amazon. The appearance of a man with a gun was enough to scatter most of the savage tribes, and the complete absence of game, except in the highlands, denied gunners an opportunity to improve their shooting. Furthermore ammunition was very expensive and exceedingly hard to procure, and most of the weapons were old-fashioned and inaccurate.

The sentinel Valdo had been brought down with a single shot, but he was a bright mark against the white foam of the river, and the rifleman had succeeded in creeping within fifty yards of him. The snipers were not to have such good fortune soon again.

CHAPTER X

A PRICE ON HER HEAD

WHEN THE SUN came up it revealed that the entire native contingent had vanished into the bush, and the portage problem presented itself again. However, while breakfast was being cooked, the little brown men began to come out of the jungle, tempted by the thought of food; and by seven o'clock camp had been struck and the outfit was again upon the move.

Les had anticipated an outbreak upon the part of his white employees; but though they grumbled among themselves, the hired men made no protest against proceeding.

"They're afraid of Gorman," Scanlon confided to Pete Holcomb. "If they kick they know he'll pay them off and send them about their business and they don't dare try to make their way back to Manáos by themselves. We're all in the pot now and we've got to stew together."

"We'll arrange our future camps differently," Pete assured him. "We present no more targets to snipers."

Scanlon laughed. "It might just as easily have been me last night as the Brazilian. The sharpshooter didn't have any prejudices. However, it was predicted years ago in Ireland that I was born to be hanged."

The party made twelve miles that day, and camped that night upon an outcropping of rocks several acres in extent which offered no hiding-place for an assassin. Next afternoon they arrived at San Gabriel, which is a miserable hamlet located upon high ground just below the beginning of the rapids.

To their surprise they found a mission at San Gabriel operated by two aged priests, whose congregation numbered a couple of score of Indians. Upon the outskirts of the village, the porters threw down their burdens and demanded to be paid and permitted to depart. No argument would change their attitude. It seemed that they feared that the priests would keep them in the place and they wanted to go back to their families.

Les offered high wages to the boat builders to remain, but these also insisted upon leaving. They would not consent to carry their loads into the village. In great disgust Les paid them, partly in *milreis* and partly in trade goods, and allowed them to leave while Dexter went into the village and called at the mission. In a short time he returned with a dozen Indians sent by the *padres*. These carried the luggage into town and stored it in an empty hut.

The mission was miserably poor, and the settlement on the verge of famine, but the priests welcomed the strangers heartily and invited the whole party to dinner. They did consent to permit the expedition to supply part of the banquet, for they had no meat, and the fishing had been poor.

DINNER, despite language difficulties, was rather gay, for a native wine proved both palatable and potent. When it was over one of the priests led Dexter to one side and talked to him long and earnestly. Dexter joined his companions with a very grave face.

"The *padre* has warned me that word has come from down river ahead of us that we are on our way to a vast forest of balata trees, and the balata hunters are gathering from all quarters. I asked him how the word came and he said one never knows. Some of his Indians gave him the information.

"He urges us to leave Louise here at the mission. He says that she would be safe, for the inhabitants of this region who are not Christians are superstitious, and the Church is a perfect sanctuary."

"Thank the *padre* for me," said Louise coldly, "and tell him nothing doing. Can you imagine me left in this appalling place alone?"

Dexter took both her hands. "Louise, dear," he said earnestly, "I wish I had never found the balata forest. The peril into which I have dragged you haunts me at night."

"Can the melodrama," said Gorman coldly. "So far the peril hasn't amounted to much—two lives lost, which we can charge up to failing to take proper precautions."

Dexter took his arm. "Look here, Les, there is something I have to tell you alone."

"You can speak in front of all of us. We're all in this mess together."

Felix shrugged his shoulders. "Very well," he said. "Louise is in especial danger. There is a big reward offered to the natives who bring her uninjured to a certain man in a certain place. Now you have it."

Louise grew very pale, and Les stepped to her side and placed his arm around her waist.

"Who is the man and where is the place?" he demanded harshly. "We'll drop our main object and take Louise to him ourselves. Let me get near the scoundrel—"

Pete was frowning reflectively. "I can't tell you the place, but I think I can name the man," he said slowly. "Aguedarno."

"Aguedarno!" exclaimed Les. "He's only after the balata."

"It's like this, Louise," said Pete. "I happen to know that South Americans, particularly Brazilians, are insane about blondes. The wise advertisers who are after Brazilian business get out calendars with pictures of beautiful blondes. Aguedarno almost toppled over when he lamped you and he didn't take his eyes off you as long as you were in the room."

"I ONLY saw the creature for a minute, Pete!" she protested.

"A minute is plenty in your case," he replied with significance.

Louise blushed unaccountably.

"Then we would be playing into his hands if I remained here," she declared. "You may be sure that there is no sanctuary which that scoundrel respects."

"I believe you are right, Pete," said Les slowly. "When I get back to Manáos I'll strangle Aguedarno with these two hands."

Dexter nodded. "Holcomb has hit it," he said. "Les, the fellow is too strong for us. The grapevine telegraph has carried his orders all over Brazil, and the jungle is full of his followers lying in wait for us. Every day's march is leading us deeper into his trap. If you ever expect to settle with Aguedarno, turn back now. We can fight our way from here to Manáos, but after we have left the river we have lost our last chance."

"Think so?" asked Les, scowling.

"I know it. The plot is evident. We stagger along, losing a man here and a man there until only you and I and Louise, or perhaps only myself and Louise, arrive at my concession. Then a band springs upon us, murders me, and drags your sister to the rendezvous with this miscreant."

"How about the balata?" asked Les coldly.

"To heck with the balata," shouted Dexter. "I'm thinking of your sister."

"Thank you, Felix," said Louise, giving him her hand. "I know that you are offering to renounce the biggest thing in your life for me."

"Dexter," said Gorman curtly, "draw me a map of the location of your concession. Take Louise and as many men as you like and go back to Manáos. I'm going to finish what I've started. I think Pete will accompany me."

"No," said Holcomb. "If Louise goes back, I go along. Manáos is Aguedarno's town, and she will need plenty of protection."

"Go, then," shouted Gorman, his face black with anger. "I'll go alone."

Louise slipped away from Dexter and stepped to her brother's side. "I wish you would stop bothering about me," she said tartly. "Where Les goes, I go."

Dexter was very white and his lips were working with

emotion. "Just remember, Gorman," he said excitedly, "that at every step I have warned you of our peril. Remember that, when your bullheadedness has brought us all to extremity."

"I'll keep it in mind," said Lester icily. "We had better turn in. Felix, why can't we march along the bank?"

"Impossible," replied Dexter. "From here on we would have to cut our way through the jungle, and we would not make a mile a day. And we would be an easy prey to savages with blow-guns."

CHAPTER XI

WITH BARE FISTS

DEXTER AND LOUISE walked toward camp, arm in arm, while Gorman detained Holcomb with a significant gesture.

"Pete," Les Gorman said frankly, "when I hired you I had a very low opinion of your courage and reliability. I consider you now my best friend and chief support. We're up against it like the devil. Enemies all around us and dependent upon a guide who has the liver of a chicken."

"Oh, come, Les! Dexter is all right."

"You know damn' well he isn't. He began to lose his nerve the night you saved him from being chucked into a rowboat on the lower Amazon. The ultimatum of Aguedarno finished him. I've been watching him and have seen his courage oozing out of him ever since.

"He was white in the gills. when the body of the Englishman was found at the first camp. He was terrified when you saved my life by potting that half-breed Lolita. He came right into the open and implored me to turn back that night they killed the Portuguese sentry, and he has just demonstrated that he is an arrant coward."

"I don't believe it," said Pete loyally. "Remember that he crossed from Colombia down to Manáos alone, and that he is noted for other explorations."

"That takes a certain amount of nerve," admitted Gorman. "I grant that he is not afraid of wild beasts and savages and ordinary dangers of travel, but he knows that beasts won't attack

Pete Holcomb leaped at the traitor in the middle of the boat.

a man unless cornered and the savages are not very formidable in this country and are easily bribed to be friendly. What gets him is the knowledge that desperate and well-armed white men are waiting to pot him from the bush. Now that doesn't bother you a bit."

Pete laughed. "Who says so? I'm in a blue funk every time I think of it."

"But you will fight like the devil and carry on to the last. I've sized you up finally."

"I don't even promise that. Dexter will fight as well as I when the pinch comes."

"Humph!" growled Gorman. "He is a welching rat, but a rat will scrap when cornered. I hate to say that about a man with whom I went to school, but I can't deny demonstrated facts. The worst of it is that Louise is in love with the fellow."

A sharp pain attacked Pete in the region of the heart.

"Has she told you so?" he stammered.

"She doesn't have to tell me. It's evident. And what infuriates me most is that he hides behind her skirts. It is 'for Louise' that he wants to turn back. He makes a grand stand play. 'To heck with the balata, her safety comes first.'"

"I believe he is sincere," said Pete.

"It's because he is convinced that we'll never get out the balata. At heart he is a quitter."

Pete was human enough to be glad that his rival was in the black books of the brother of Louise, but he was too decent to join in the denunciation of Dexter.

"That remains to be demonstrated," he replied.

"You certainly are from Missouri," retorted Gorman. "Pete, that man is no husband for Louise. I won't have it!"

"As I told you in New York," said Pete coldly, "Louise will marry whom she chooses when she chooses."

"Now, if she had only fallen in love with you!" said Les regretfully.

"Do you remember what you told me about that in New York?" demanded Pete angrily.

"I didn't realize what kind of man you were, Pete."

"I'm no better than I was then."

"Well, I'm just a bum judge of humans. I would hare sworn that Felix was a go-through guy."

"I promised you that Louise would not fall in love with me. She hasn't. If she happened to, now, would you oppose our marriage?"

"You just put that up to me, will you?" demanded Les eagerly.

Pete grinned. "If I can, I will. I've been crazy about Louise since the minute she came into the room that day you hired me. Now would you like to hear something about yourself?"

"Go as far as you like," replied Gorman good-naturedly.

"**YOU** are a big, thick-headed, mule-eared wild boar," Pete began. "For no reason in the world you have dragged us all into this horrible mess, and you are too stubborn to admit you made a mistake."

"You're wrong! I admit it, but I'm going through." Gorman was flushing.

"As a result of your lack of human intelligence, you are going to get us all killed. You know your sister will stick to you no matter what happens, and you ought to be decent enough to quit for her sake; but not you. You are incrusted with jackass pride—"

"Pete," said Gorman softly, "one word more, and I'll bust you in the jaw."

"You're a big, balky—"

Wham!

The two men were facing each other and only two feet apart. The big fist of Gorman slammed against the jaw of Pete Holcomb, though not on the button. Pete went down, but not out. With a snarl he dived at Gorman's legs and brought him to the ground. He was upon him and crashing hard blows into his face with all the pent-up resentment of a subordinate who had been obeying fool orders from a man who had rubbed him the wrong way from the first.

Pete was not a pugilist, however, and his blows were not powerful enough to give the quietus to a bigger and stronger man. Les rolled him off and got to his feet. Pete came charging in, weeping with anger and both fists flying. Gorman measured him with his left and slammed through his right to the point of the jaw. Curtains for Mr. Holcomb.

When he came to, his head was lying upon Gorman's knee and the big man was wiping his face with a handkerchief dipped in cold river water.

"How are you feeling?" asked Les pleasantly.

"All right," said Pete with a grin.

"What a fighting fool you are!" remarked Les. "Why don't you take somebody your size?"

"You hit me first, you big stiff."

"Kid, I stood more hard names from you than I ever took from any man. I gave you fair warning to stop, and you kept on. Had enough?"

"You bet," admitted Holcomb. "Well, it was worth a licking to tell you the truth about yourself."

Les grinned. "I guess there was some truth in your charges. Pete, are we friends?"

"I suppose so," said Pete, smiling.

"Then get up and let me tell you something. I think things out in my dull way. I believe with you that Aguedarno is after Louise. I observed the way the beast looked at her that day in my room in Manáos. Felix says the woods are full of his assassins. I believe that, too. I have had evidence of it.

"Well, if he wants Louise, we are simply giving her to him if we turn back. He won't allow one of us to reach Manáos alive. Our only hope is fighting through to the Colombian border and coming out on the Caribbean at some Colombian port. I'm not thinking about the balata at all. Have not, since I heard that the scoundrel coveted my sister. Now do you understand me?"

"Gee, I've been a darn fool," sighed Pete Holcomb.

"Furthermore, I'm not going to give Aguedarno the satisfaction of locating the balata fields. I'm satisfied that we couldn't get the stuff out through Manáos in sufficient quantity to pay. I've got an idea about that which remains to be worked out, but not a word to Dexter."

"Les," said Pete slowly, "I've been thinking for a week that it's too bad you didn't have my brains. But I don't know anything."

"You know plenty," said Gorman. "Sorry I had to hit you. Let's go to bed."

"One thing, chief. Why not explain your plan to your sister and Dexter? Lou is so loyal that she sticks by you even when you make it appear that you set this balata concession above her safety."

"Pete," demanded Les compassionately, "Felix is scared to death now, but without him we would be babes in the woods. How long do you suppose he would stick if he thought that there was nothing in it for him, not even the forlorn hope of making good his balata concession?"

"Then tell Louise."

"She is in love with Dexter, I tell you. I can't depend upon her keeping the thing a secret."

"Then how are you going to explain to Dexter that we are not bound for his concession?"

Les grinned. "Things will probably be made so hot for us in the next few weeks that he'll suggest we make a bee-line for safety across the Colombian frontier and leave the balata for another season."

PETE went soberly to his blankets. His jaw ached, but he didn't mind that, for he had a peep into the workings of the mind of a really big man. Les, whom he had accused of being a stubborn jackass, whom he had practically taxed with risking his sister's life for gain, had worked things out correctly in his own mind and planned accordingly. If Aguedarno was plotting to capture Louise, it would have been the height of folly to go over the back trail to Manáos. Either the men would be picked off from ambush or they would be clapped into a jail in some rotten town and accused of the murder of Pao Lolita. In either case Louise would be left without a protector.

But Aguedarno wanted balata even more than he wanted to lay his hands on Louise Gorman. Could they get through into civilized Colombia? Dexter had stated that only half a dozen persons had ever succeeded in traveling across country from Manáos to Bogotá, but Dexter himself was one of them. With him to guide and Les Gorman to command, they had a chance, though a slim one. None of the other explorers had a forest full of white enemies to lay snares for them.

What a wonderful chap old Lester was! Pete could understand now how he had won through to millions in the State of Nevada. It was great that Lester was for him strong. It made Pete feel that there was a man inside himself. He was glad he had nerve enough to attack a bigger and stronger man even though he received a beating. And Les had complimented him in the highest manner when he said he wished that it was Pete Holcomb and not Felix Dexter that Louise loved.

Back in New York Louise had liked him a lot, but, mindful of his promise to her brother, he had been careful not to display his feelings for her. And Dexter had come along, a big out-of-doors man, and carried the child off her feet. Of course she swallowed whole his yarn about wanting to call off the expedition for her sake. A man in love would act like that. To do Dexter justice it probably had a lot to do with his attitude. Pete couldn't believe him as yellow as Les declared. He was still impressed by the man's record.

CHAPTER XII

CATASTROPHE

THE NIGHT PASSED quietly as did several other nights in San Gabriel. It was evident that their enemies did not care to show their hand in a place where there would be impressive witnesses to their evil deeds.

During the ten days that the Gorman expedition spent at San Gabriel no white man showed his face, but the mission Indians reported that several parties had passed in the night upon the opposite side of the rapids. Gorman assumed them to be balata hunters, probably minions of Aguedarno who were taking advantage of the delay to get into the up river country first.

Dexter, having made up his mind that the die was cast, worked with a will and forced the two experienced boat build-ers and their clumsy assistants to work faster than they consid-ered necessary. Scanlon and the German, who knew something of carpentering, pitched in with white men's tools and speeded up what was looking like a month's job.

On the tenth day the little fleet was dragged a couple of miles up river and launched. Because of the swiftness of the river current it was necessary to proceed close to the bank whose trees provided grateful shade, but housed serpents, hornets, and tree ants, most annoying of all.

Les, Pete, Dexter and Louise each commanded a boat. Scanlon and the German were assigned to Louise's *montería*. One of the hired adventurers was placed with each of the other three principals; Gorman thought it best to prevent their followers from clustering together in one boat and, perhaps, deserting.

Dexter had explained that they must follow the Rio Negro for several hundred miles until it became the border between Colombia and Brazil and at a small tributary without a name they would turn into Colombia, follow that stream for another hundred miles, and strike into the jungle for a short distance to the balata forest.

He also explained that at the mouths of various tributaries ahead there were settlements whose Brazilian chiefs might have orders to pounce upon them; therefore they must plan to pass these danger spots at night, if it were possible to persuade the rowers to work after darkness had descended upon the river.

ON THE SIXTH morning the rowers upon the *montería* of Dexter, who led the way, headed toward a barren point which jutted into the river and despite his protests beached the boat. The others followed the example of the first *montería*.

They dared go no farther, they informed Dexter. They would build themselves dugouts and go down river in them while the white men must procure rowers from the chief of the Angoni tribe upon the borders of whose country they had arrived. They agreed to send a messenger bearing gifts to the chief if the white men would remain to protect them until they had constructed their dugout canoes.

Three days they spent upon that sandy spit, the natives cutting down small trees and hewing out twelve-foot logs.

On the third day the chief of the Angoni arrived in person. He was tall for a Rio Negro savage, with brawny arms, spindly legs and the pot belly of all natives, caused probably by an almost exclusive diet of farina. He was followed by two-score of his subjects and stopped at a distance of a hundred feet from the camp. The chief, like his men, was stark naked save for a G-string and parrakeet feathers in his long black hair. He carried a tall stick which the whites assumed to be a blow-gun, but which turned out to be his staff of office. This he thrust into the sand.

His army carried crude spears and six-foot sticks which proved to be hollow tubes through which they blew short darts, the ends of which were dipped in poison. The white men shuddered as they identified the things, while the natives looked with awe at the rifles that the members of the invading expedition significantly displayed.

However, the visit was pacific. The chief came to find out how much it was worth to him to supply rowers. His followers jeered at the mission Indians who turned almost white with fright and huddled for protection behind the white men.

One of the Christian Indians acted as interpreter and Dexter laid upon the ground between the two forces what he offered as wages; machetes, sheath knives, beads and colored cotton cloth. The chief demanded twice what was displayed and compromised upon half as much again. He wished to be paid in advance, but consented to take half now and wait until his boatmen returned for the other half. Twenty-four men would report for duty in the morning, he informed them.

It was quite a businesslike meeting. As for Pete Holcomb, the blow-gun of the savage had been his strongest deterrent against the trip up the Amazon and he had not supposed that treaties could be arranged with these primitive men. From the moment of the visit of the Angoni, he wasted no more thought upon poisoned darts—which was rather premature of him.

Immediately after the departure of the Angoni, the mission Indians piled into their dugouts and made off with their wages. They did not even wave good-by. That night Gorman ordered double watch lest the savages decide to attack the camp and capture all the trade goods instead of a small portion of them.

If the idea had occurred to the chief, the presence of so many guns deterred him and the night passed peacefully. With the dawn, appeared more than two-score conscripts who, to the concern of the whites, brought their terrifying weapons with them.

"We'll collect the weapons when we get under way," said Dexter. "They carry them for their own protection on the return trip. Once a chief has made an agreement you can usually depend upon his keeping it."

LOUISE was the first to protest against the division of the party as required by the *monterías*.

"You don't have to worry about Scanlon," she told Lester. "He is as loyal as possible, but he's dull company. Let him be placed in charge of my boat and I'll come in with you, Les."

"Or with me," suggested Dexter eagerly.

Pete said nothing, but he dared not look at Louise lest she see the longing in his eyes.

"You think the Irishman is reliable, don't you, Pete?" asked Gorman.

"The best man we have," he replied.

"All right, Lou. Shift into my boat in the morning. Everybody to bed."

More dreary days passed, humid and monotonous. Not even an Indian fisherman was visible on the river, which had narrowed to about three-quarters of a mile. Far to the west they could discern the blue peaks of very high mountains, the foothills of the Andes, but the river was now flowing from north to south. They were within a few score miles of the equator.

There was no persuading of the Angoni rowers to go on after the sun went down and they had to pass a big settlement, which Dexter said was the last outpost of Brazilian rubber planting, in mid afternoon. Though a score of natives appeared on the shore and waved to them to put in, Dexter kept the boatmen at work and they soon left the place behind. While there were several boats drawn up on the beach, no attempt was made to send out a boat to ask them their news and their business.

Some six or eight miles farther up river they arrived at a camping place and went through the usual business of settling down for the night.

Holcomb slept badly. Insects got under his mosquito screens and buzzed around his ears. Scanlon lay snoring beside him. With a snort of disgust he crawled out of the little tent and crept to the fire where a sentinel was supposed to keep a smudge going. There was a smudge, but the wind had shifted and it was blowing out to the river.

There was no moon, but there was a very faint glow from the stream. Pete crawled into the smudge smoke which choked him but drove off the pestiferous insects. He saw Dexter seated with his back against a tent, his rifle across his knees, some thirty feet distant. Felix had observed Pete and waved a hand to him. The surviving Brazilian, the former clerk of the Central Hotel at Manáos, sat on a stump within a few feet of the water. His profile was toward the river, his eyes on the jungle.

The very light breeze shifted and the smudge blew toward the tents again and Holcomb could discern the four *monterías* which floated in deep water within a couple of feet of the bank and were made fast by lines to small bushes. He could see nothing distinctly; the boats were black shadows on the river.

Was he mistaken, or was there something moving on one of the boats? He peered through the darkness and assumed he was mistaken. No, the boat was coming closer to the shore as if the line was being hauled in. Its clumsy prow bumped noiselessly against the bank.

It was very strange to have the heavy boat moving against the current. Perhaps a manatee, one of the huge sea cows which live in the river, had come up under it and given it a push; but in that case there would be ripples on the black water and the beast would have made a splash. It was very strange.

Crack!

There was a blinding flash from the bow of the *montería*, the report of a heavy revolver, and the Brazilian sentinel toppled off the stump.

WITH an oath Pete jumped to his feet, narrowly escaping a bullet from the rifle of Felix Dexter. In a few bounds he was at the river bank and he saw a man slash the mooring line with a knife with one hand while he thrust the boat away from shore with the other.

In a couple of seconds there were four feet of black water, filled with horrible things, between shore and boat; but Pete Holcomb didn't think of that. He was flying through the air and landed on a rower's bench in the prow with such force that he plunged forward against the form of the assassin, who had risen to meet him, knife in hand.

The man fell backward into the bottom of the boat with Holcomb on top and there ensued a desperate struggle in the *montería* which was gripped by the current and dragged rapidly down stream.

The fellow was half naked and so was Holcomb. The man was desperate, but no more so than Pete, who remembered too late that he had, without a weapon of his own, charged a murderer, armed with gun and knife. Pete had a momentary advantage from being above his opponent, who also had had most of the breath knocked out of his body; but the man still clutched his knife and endeavored to use it. They were both like blind men because of the darkness. Breast against breast, they fought silently and viciously.

Holcomb was a big man with much latent strength, though his muscles, despite the hard labor of the past few weeks, were underdeveloped. His antagonist was smaller, but wiry and powerful, and the fellow quickly regained his wind.

The knife swished past Pete's left ear as the man beneath him struck out blindly with it. Pete grasped for the knife-arm, but it eluded him. Another vicious stab grazed his shoulder as Holcomb drove a clenched right fist into the man's face.

The knife-wielder rolled Pete half off of him, shifted his grip on the knife, and, getting under Pete's left arm, thrust with all his strength at the body. Holcomb was twisting, however, and landed in the bottom of the boat beside his enemy. The knife was driven for several inches into the hard wood of the side of the boat where it resisted the effort of the murderer to pull it out.

Realizing his advantage, the American pummeled the man's face, but his position prevented the blows from doing more than annoy his foe. The man abandoned the knife and fastened both his claws in Pete's throat.

His hands were strong and his grip could not be broken. Desperately Holcomb slammed fists into stomach and against his chin. He was being strangled; his destiny was to die in the bottom of a boat in the middle of the Rio Negro, choked to death by a filthy murderer. By heaven, no!

Pete brought up his knee against the groin of his enemy with such force that the man's breath hissed out of him and he moaned with pain, but he kept his death grip. Again and again Pete worked his knee, but his strength was oozing from him. He pulled with both hands at the wrists of steel and jabbed his knee into the fellow's stomach. In another minute he would be through.

But his antagonist could not resist the gruelling pain of the American's knee in his abdomen. With a tortured curse he let go of Pete's throat, turned, rose upon his knees and plunged for the spot where he had dropped his revolver when he drew his knife to cut the mooring.

PETE was unexpectedly free. He drew in a deep breath, staggered to his feet, and fell upon the fellow's back as he was reaching for the gun which lay on a rower's bench. As the man grasped it, Pete Holcomb's fingers gripped his throat from behind. And his superior weight crushed the murderer down upon the bench. With each second Pete's strength returned.

The assassin pointed the weapon over his shoulder and pulled the trigger. A bullet whizzed past Holcomb's ear. He squeezed tighter. The man, who was now getting a taste of his own garroting, in desperation tried to place the muzzle against Holcomb's side. But to do so he had to twist his arm backward, and Pete let go the throat, grasped the wrist and twisted the arm.

A shriek of pain revealed how the man was suffering. Holcomb pressed his advantage, caught the arm with both hands, knocked the gun out of the relaxed grasp and threw all his weight upon the arm. *Crack!* He had broken the fellow's right arm.

Shocked, Pete let go. The injured man, moaning and growling, drew back, swung round and dived for the gun which lay on the bottom of the boat between them. Pete hooked his right and knocked the fellow backward, then he himself stooped and picked up the revolver.

With a snarl the man jumped the bench and grasped the haft of the knife with his left hand. He pressed his foot against the planking and pulled. The knife came out and he turned like a wolf at bay.

"Drop it!" warned Pete. Instead, the fellow came for him. Holcomb lifted his weapon and fired point-blank at him. The man crumpled and fell with a crash. The battle was over.

Weak and trembling, Pete collapsed upon a seat and the weapon dropped from his nerveless fingers. His enemy neither moved nor moaned. The American had taken no aim at that distance, but the bullet had entered the body and probably had penetrated the heart.

Pete breathed heavily and stared remorsefully at the black shape in the bottom of the *montería*. Of course the man deserved to die. He had shot the Brazilian sentry in cold blood, and would have slain Holcomb. He was a filthy murderer, but Pete was no killer and it was horrible to have his victim, so near, mutely reproaching him.

Who was he? How did he happen to be hiding in one of Gorman's *monterías?* How had he crept into camp? Where did he come from?

Pete remembered that there were cigarettes and matches in the cabin of each *montería*. He ought to have a look at the man and he ought to search him. He might have on his person papers which would incriminate Aguedarno.

As he climbed over benches toward the cabin at the stern

he saw, far up the river upon the right bank a pin point of light which twinkled and went out as he gazed. Then he was groping about in the cabin and finally laid hands on a box of matches.

With much distaste he returned to the bow, scratched a match and allowed its light to fall upon the dead man's face. He uttered an exclamation of astonishment. He was gazing down upon John Barnes, one of the members of the expedition, an American sailor who was on the bank at Manáos and whom Dexter had hired confidently as unlikely to be in the pay of Aguedarno.

Barnes was not the sort to inspire confidence. He was a mean-looking, dissipated, untrustworthy specimen of seafaring man, but his nationality had been his chief recommendation to the Gorman expedition.

"I'll be damned!" exclaimed Pete. "Why, you dirty traitor, I'm glad I shot you. One of our own people and you sold us out! Let's see what you've got on your person."

Nothing was revealed by a search of the late John Barnes, who was clad in shirt and trousers and was barefooted.

A GUST of fury shook Holcomb. "I won't have you in the boat with me, dead or alive," he shouted.

He lifted the corpse and threw it overboard with a shudder. Then he awoke to his own situation. He was in the middle of the river, being carried away from camp by the swift current as fast as a man could run. He had removed his outer garments when he lay down that night, was barefoot, possessed not even his watch.

However, the shots had awakened the camp and Gorman would immediately launch a pursuing boat. He was all right. He only had a few minutes start on his friends. The thing to do, though, was to get the *montería* out of the current and tie up to the bank, keep a watch and when the rescue craft hove in sight, give them a halloo and put out into the stream. He fumbled around and found one of the long sweeps, put it out and tried to edge the craft toward the left bank a half mile distant. It was slow work and he had no means of judging what progress he was making.

He had ample opportunity during the next hour to consider the state of affairs of the party's situation and his spirits grew very low.

There were ten men and one woman when they landed from the yacht "Louise Gorman." The Englishman had been murdered at the first camp. The Brazilian Valdo had been shot from ambush after leaving Pao Lolita's. Now the unfortunate hotel clerk had been killed or wounded and Barnes had come to a bad end. Four of the seven hired men had been eliminated in one way or another. The party was reduced from eleven rifles including Louise's to seven including himself.

That was a war of attrition with a vengeance; Aguedarno was lopping them off, one by one. Of those who remained, Scanlon was to be depended upon, the German cook was probably all right; but Lawson, the other American, had been with Barnes when Dexter found the pair in a Manáos water front saloon. Lawson might be tarred with the same brush.

The *montería* was much too unwieldy to be handled by one man. What had Barnes intended to do?

Pete thought that his plan was to drop downstream with the current and steer the boat ashore at the settlement they had passed, some ten or twelve miles below the camp. Most likely he had started from Manáos with orders to kill one of the party and steal a boat at just that point. On this *montería* were eight or nine hundred pounds of freight whose loss would be as severe a blow to the expedition as the loss of a human life. It was a diabolical plot, but only part of it had succeeded.

It seemed to him that an hour must have passed and he did not appear to have drawn any closer to the left bank. Pete had no knowledge of boats and no experience with oars, but it occurred to him that his sweep used as a rudder might be more effective than it was at present, so he carried it to the stern.

The current in the middle of the river was so strong that it eddied and bubbled, but some minutes elapsed before he could discover that he was having any effect upon the course of the big boat. Very, very slowly he began to edge toward the left, but the dawn came up and found him still several hundred yards from shore.

CHAPTER XIII

PURSUIT

THE GUNFIRE AT the camp awoke the sleeping members. Gorman, rifle in hand, plunged out of his tent to find Dexter standing on the bank staring into the darkness.

"What happened?" demanded Les sharply.

Still staring downstream Dexter pointed to the still form lying on the shore.

"One more gone, probably two," he said dolefully. He was already surrounded by the other men and Louise, and the Indians had leaped from the ground and were chattering like shrill monkeys.

"It's the clerk," said Les, stooping over the sentry. "Shot through the head and finished. Who else?"

Dexter placed a despondent hand to his forehead.

"Holcomb, no doubt, and one of our *monterías.*"

"Pete gone!" exclaimed Louise wildly. "Oh, oh! Is he dead? How do you know?"

Les's hand came down heavily upon Dexter's shoulder.

"Pull yourself together and explain what happened," he commanded sternly.

"I was sitting in front of my tent, wide awake," said Dexter. "I saw Pete crawl out of his tent and get into the smoke from the smudge. The clerk was posted on the bank. I waved a hand to Pete and he waved back. A few minutes later a shot came from one of our own *monterías* and the Brazilian fell over.

"Holcomb, like a fool, let out a yell and rushed for the boat.

The fellow on board had slipped the moorings and she was sliding away from the bank, but Pete made a flying leap and landed on the boat. I fired at the flash of the assassin's gun, but Holcomb came into my line of vision and I had to hold my fire. I dared not shoot when he landed on the boat for fear that I should hit him. The *montería* was out of sight in a few seconds."

"Man a boat and we'll pursue," commanded Gorman.

"I say, Mr. Gorman," exclaimed Scanlon. "Barnes is missing. He isn't in his tent and he ain't here."

"Well, we know where Holcomb is," retorted Gorman. "Grab Louise, Felix! She's fainted! First time she ever did that in her life."

Dexter caught the girl in his arms and ran with her to her tent, carried her in and laid her tenderly on her blankets—for not even Louise had a cot.

When he returned a moment later, Gorman was endeavoring to instruct the natives to man a boat, but his pantomime was not understood by them. Dexter grasped his arm.

"It's no use. Nothing will induce them to put out on the river," he declared.

"Then we'll go after him ourselves."

"It takes four expert rowers, preferably six, to operate a big *montería*."

"Well, there are five of us."

"But we can't leave the camp in the hands of the Indians; they would steal everything and be gone when we returned."

"Damn it, man, Holcomb is on that boat with the assassin."

"And probably dead by now," replied Dexter soberly. "I don't think he had a weapon—Listen!"

From down river came the report of a shot, faintly but distinct. They strained their ears and a moment later heard a second shot and then nothing more.

"**THAT'S** the end of Holcomb," said Dexter. "He tackled the murderer and was drilled, the fool."

Gorman lifted his big fist toward heaven. "We'll find out. Drive those swine into the boats."

"They won't go. It is a superstition not to go on the river at night. Devils are abroad."

"Then you and I will take a boat—"

"And leave Louise without one of us, with what you know about Aguedarno's intentions toward her?"

Gorman gnashed his teeth. Dexter's logic was unanswerable and for the moment he hated him for it.

"Beg pardon," said Scanlon at his elbow. "Barnes certainly isn't in the camp. I think that it was him that shot the Brazilian and swiped the *montería*."

"That's it," exclaimed Dexter. "The fellow was an agent of Aguedarno's."

"But he was an American," protested Gorman.

"And a dirty hound, if I may say so," declared Scanlon. "Anyway he ain't here. You were on guard, Mr. Dexter. Did you see him at all?"

"No," said Dexter. "That means, Les, that we have lost four men—five, if we include Holcomb, and we might as well include him. Those shots were the end of him."

"I'm going to find out," declared Gorman doggedly.

"Les," pleaded Felix. "Realize our situation. We have Louise to think about. Scanlon is all right, but can we trust the others? Dare we leave Louise in their care?"

"I can care for myself," asserted Louise, who had emerged from her tent and rejoined them. "Les, we've got to find Pete, haven't we?"

Dexter spread out his arms in a gesture of despair. "If he is alive, it's up to him to find his own way back," he declared. "Louise, Pete lost his head. He jumped on that boat without a weapon. We heard the shots which killed him when you were unconscious. It's useless."

Tears were streaming down the girl's face.

"He's our friend," she cried. "And it was heroic of him to attack an armed murderer with his bare hands. I'll never speak to either of you again if yon don't start right out after him."

"Great Scott," cried Dexter, "I'm as anxious as you are, but Pete is a city man, no match for a woodsman in a rough and tumble. That fellow Barnes was a powerful little brute and he had a gun."

"I'm afraid Felix is right," said Gorman who placed a big arm around his sister's shoulder. "Pete didn't have a chance. It was heroic, but poor judgment. Three of our men are dead, Barnes has deserted and probably killed Holcomb. For heaven's sake, Lou, don't cry like that."

She had buried her face on his bosom and her body was racked with heavy sobs.

"Nevertheless," he continued, "it's our duty to go after him. We may at least punish the murderer and recover the *montería*."

"Les," replied Dexter, "the river is a mile wide and black as pitch. That boat has already been carried by the current a mile or two down the stream. You might pass within a hundred feet of it and not see it, but the scoundrel Barnes, who is drifting, will hear our oars and may drill one or two of us before we know that he is in the vicinity."

"Let me take a boat and one man," said Scanlon. "We'll go faster than he can. If we capture the boat we'll run the two of them up to the bank and the rest of you can come down when it's daylight and pick us up. Of course we couldn't get back by ourselves."

DEXTER considered this proposition for a moment.

"You would miss Barnes, or he would hear you first and shoot you before you knew you were upon him, and we'd lose two *monterías* and two men whom we can't spare."

"All right," said Gorman sullenly. "What do you propose, Felix?"

"It's only a couple of hours to dawn. If, by a miracle, Holcomb is alive and in control of the boat he will steer it to the bank and tie up. He will calculate that we know he can't row it up-stream and he will expect us to come after him.

"At dawn we shall go in a body and travel very fast down-stream with our rowers. We can even overtake Barnes, assuming he hasn't landed at that settlement which we avoided yesterday."

"Barnes is a tough egg," said Scanlon. "If Mr. Holcomb didn't have a gun he had no chance. We heard two shots. The first was when Barnes dropped him and the second when he found that the kid was only wounded and he finished him off."

"Do something!" screamed Louise who began to beat her brother's breast with her clenched fists. "Do something! Do something!"

"I'm afraid he is right," said Lester slowly. "If Pete is gone, Louise, it means that we must guard the living even more carefully. It would be suicide to divide our forces. Holcomb is smart and if he happens to have overcome that scoundrel Barnes, he will reason just as Dexter does. He will steer to the bank, tie up and wait for us to come down at daylight. We'll set about breaking camp and be ready to start at the first streak of dawn."

"Do something now!" commanded Louise hysterically.

"Miss," said Scanlon, "those shots meant that either Holcomb killed Barnes or Barnes killed him. It's all over, one way or the other. If Holcomb won, he'll be waiting for us in the morning. If he lost, well, we'll flay Barnes alive."

"Please be reasonable, Lou," pleaded her brother.

She heaved a deep sigh. "All right," she said in a low tone. "I'll control myself."

The two hours dragged horribly, but the sky finally began to grow light and the savage rowers consented to board the three remaining boats. The expedition was under way before the sun actually showed himself and while the western sky was still black and stars shone brightly in that direction.

With the aid of the swift current they traveled fast. In an

hour they passed the settlement from which it had taken them nearly four hours to row upstream to their camp.

In three hours they were fully thirty-five miles below their starting point, despite the tendency of the rowers to loaf, and their eyes were weary from the strain of staring at the river banks in hope of spying the nose of a *montería* poking out from the shore.

"The matter seems to be settled," said Dexter miserably. "Barnes shot him, threw him overboard and put into that village up above."

"Then we'll pull him out of the village," retorted Gorman. "I liked that kid, Felix. I was responsible for dragging him into this wilderness. He had more common sense than both of us put together, and the nerve of the devil. I'll catch the dog that killed him and I'll hang him to the nearest tree. I—I'd like to torture him."

The three *monterías* had drawn together for a conference. The natives rested on their sweeps and gazed impassively at their white masters. The three white employees listened eagerly.

"Keep your head," Dexter pleaded. "We can't bust into that village. We would be outnumbered ten to one and Barnes may not have taken refuge there."

"That's something we're going to find out," retorted Gorman. "There are five of us—"

"Six," Louise corrected him.

"Right, Lou. Six good men, if one of them is a girl. We're well armed. Every man's hand is against us in this jungle and we might as well show them now as any time that we can strike back. Men, are you with me?"

"You bet, boss," shouted Scanlon. "If that skunk is there we'll get him and skin him."

"Tell the rowers to return upstream," commanded Gorman. Dexter shook his head dubiously, but gave the order.

CHAPTER XIV

DUBIOUS WELCOME

THE EXPEDITION ARRIVED off the settlement a half hour before sunset. The place had been a big rubber plantation in its time and a quay had been built at which launches and small craft could tie up. In the dusk they observed two or three *monterías* at the pier and a dozen dugout canoes. Land had been cleared for a score of acres and a long, low, comfortable-looking house stood on a rise of ground a hundred yards back from the river, while behind it and at either side were warehouses and a huddle of native huts.

The sound of their oars before they came around a bend in the river had been heard in the settlement and men, women, and children were running down to the water's edge. Most of them were naked natives, but Gorman observed three or four men in dirty whites in the throng.

"Tie up to the pier, land in a body, and demand to talk with the boss and nobody else," he instructed.

"Les, I implore you not to be highhanded," said Felix. "Remember Pao Lolita."

"If they are sheltering the murderer I'll burn their damned settlement," Gorman growled. "A lot of water has passed under bridges since Pete shot that greasy Negro who was about to murder me. Now, men, and you, Louise, keep close together, have your rifles ready and don't allow anybody to separate us."

Their landing was unopposed and they grouped on the quay.

A halfbreed came forward, bowing from the waist and scraping the ground with his straw hat.

"Welcome," he said in Portuguese. "We saw you pass up river yesterday and we are wondering how you come again to Isonzo from down river."

"We shall explain that to your chief," said Dexter. "Please ask him if we may speak to him."

"As I said, you are welcome. You will camp here to-night, of course."

"We are in a great hurry."

"But you must remain here overnight. Your Indians will refuse to go farther," said the Portuguese, smiling.

"I don't see our boat among those tied up here," said Les in a low tone to his sister. "Do you?"

"No, positively not."

"Of course they would hide it. What does he say, Felix?"

"Invites us to camp here, and we've got to. It's getting dark."

"Then we'll camp right here on the beach where we can watch our stuff. Is the headman coming?"

Dexter talked with the Portuguese.

"Dom Manuel Parama lives in the big house," he said. "He sends word that he is delighted to have us as his guests and invites us to dinner."

"Declined with thanks. Ask him if he has seen anything of a lone American in a *montería*."

"No *montería* has passed here today," replied Dexter after putting the question.

"For the good reason that it put in here," muttered Les.

"It is very discourteous to decline the invitation and we may be wrong in our suspicion. This fellow insists that we go up to the house. He will be responsible for our goods."

"And who'll be responsible for him?" asked Scanlon with a grin.

"Make camp at the head of the quay," commanded Gorman.

"Dexter, you and I will go to the house and question the fellow. Scanlon, you're in charge. If we are not back in half an hour, rush the place."

"I'll go with you," declared Louise.

"Please remain here, dear. Your rifle may be needed."

"Very well," she said meekly.

"I'd go alone, Felix," said Les, "except that your Portuguese is necessary."

"I understand."

DEXTER gave the order to the Indians to set up tents and build fires, telling Scanlon to be closely on guard. Then he walked with Gorman and the Portuguese up the path which led to the big house.

No word was spoken as they mounted rotting and creaking steps and crossed a porch, the boards of which threatened to give way beneath their feet. An Indian in a white costume opened the door and led them into what had been an imposing drawing-room where Dom Manuel Parama sat in a big chair, affecting to read by the light of a kerosene lamp.

He rose, bowed, and came forward with outstretched hand.

"It is my pleasure to welcome my American guests," he declared effusively.

"How do you know that we are Americans?" demanded Dexter.

"Word of your progress up river has preceded you, gentlemen. But where is the rest of your party, including the young lady?"

"We wished to talk with you first," replied Dexter.

Parama bowed again. He was a spare, swarthy man with burning black eyes, white hair and an iron-gray goatee.

"I am at your service, gentlemen," he replied. "My house is yours."

"We are seeking a murderer, one of our men who shot a comrade, stole a *montería* and set off alone in it last night. An American named Barnes."

"What a scoundrel!" ejaculated Dom Manuel. "I regret that he has not fallen into my hands. I am the magistrate of this province."

"Tell him we know he is here and that he must give him up or we'll burn the house over his head," said Gorman savagely.

The Portuguese understood it as a threat from his tone, and his eyes flashed.

"The *senhor* appears to be angry," he said softly. "He does not appear to understand that I have offered to him my hospitality."

"One of his best friends was killed," replied Dexter apologetically. "You appreciate that he is distraught."

"I sympathize with him. My home is not what it used to be, but I can give you gentlemen and the lady bedrooms. Your men are accustomed to sleep on the ground, no doubt. Anyway, I have not room for them. Your names, gentlemen?"

"I beg your pardon. I should have introduced Senhor Lester Gorman. I am named Dexter. We are on a hunting and exploring trip."

"Word has come to that effect," replied Dom Manuel.

Dexter repeated the invitation and Gorman shook his head.

"It may be kindly meant and it may be a scheme to separate the party. Until I know whether he is hiding the murderer I want none of his hospitality."

"If you will permit us to spend the night near our boats," said Dexter to the Brazilian, "we shall not impose upon you further. We are all too tired for a dinner party."

"As you will," replied Dom Manuel. "I regret not to have the pleasure of your company."

The Americans returned his bow and left the house.

"What do you think?" asked Gorman.

"He was effusively hospitable and exceedingly courteous, but so is the vilest brigand in this country. I am inclined to think that he isn't shielding Barnes, but it is possible."

"It's a big place," said Les thoughtfully. "And it's dark already. If we did make a search it would be easy to keep him out of sight."

"The fact that he received two armed men alone is a point in his favor. It looks as though he had a dozen Brazilians and a half hundred Indians about the plantation. We had better spend the night here and depart without making trouble in the morning. We are hopelessly outnumbered," Dexter pointed out.

THEY FOUND camp made and a fire going when they returned. The boatmen had camped a couple of hundred feet distant and were already swinishly devouring their fish and farina.

Louise met them with an anxious face.

"Any news?" she demanded.

"No," replied Lester. "We were politely received by a gentlemanly old *hidalgo* who wanted to wine and dine us and put us up for the night. I thought it best to refuse. Dexter, we three will sit up all night and get some sleep in the boats to-morrow."

The white people ate a frugal meal and sat around in a circle for an hour afterward, sorrowfully discussing the good qualities of Peter Holcomb. His sense of humor, his cheerfulness, the ability he had to make fun of his own discomfort, had endeared him to the men as well as the chiefs of the expedition.

"There were lads like him in my regiment in the war," said Scanlon. "They were rich and never done a stroke of work in their lives and when they took a bath they used scented soap. Say, those lads stood the trenches better than lots of us who had done hard labor all our years. They sort of made a game of it and cracked jokes that kept us all in fine fettle. Pete was like that."

Louise listened and said nothing, but every now and then a tear rolled down her cheek. Dexter occasionally reached for her hand and pressed it sympathetically and she allowed him to retain it for minutes at a time, which did not escape the watchful eye of her brother.

"When he turned up in New York," Gorman told Dexter, "I remembered him as an irresponsible, good-natured idler. I engaged him as my secretary because he was a kid you couldn't help but like, but I didn't think he had anything to him. I thought he was—"

"You said he was part monkey, part donkey," said Louise reproachfully.

"I ate my words long ago. I had a talk with him a few nights back and I had a chance to tell him that I was for him a hundred per cent. I'm certainly glad he learned how he stood with me before this happened."

"I'll never forget what he did for me on the Amazon steamer," said Dexter sadly. "Say, Les, there's something doing in the settlement."

Gorman jumped to his feet and stared toward the house in which all lights had suddenly been extinguished.

"There is a body of men creeping toward us," he exclaimed. "They are crawling on their bellies. Get your rifles, men, flat on the ground. Don't fire until I give the word. Kick out that camp fire."

He obeyed his own order by dashing at the fire and kicking the embers in all directions.

A sharp cry came from the darkness.

"They ask a parley," cried Dexter excitedly. "What shall I say?"

"Tell them not to come a foot nearer, and to let their leader approach. We promise not to shoot him."

Dexter shouted these conditions in Portuguese and a moment later an extraordinary figure came out of the darkness.

It was Dom Manuel Parama, dressed in a uniform of green and gold of an ancient cut, topped by a cocked hat with a red ostrich feather in it. By his side hung a sword and in his hand was a pistol.

"I am returning your visit," he said.

"In state, I perceive," replied Dexter. "What is your purpose?"

"You are surrounded by fifty well armed men," replied Parama. "If that does not deter you, we have a machine gun. Your situation is hopeless. I advise you to surrender."

"This is your hospitality," reproached Dexter.

PARAMA waved his hand airily. "You refused it. If you refuse to surrender I implore you to permit the young woman to pass through our lines to the house, for a machine gun has no eyes."

"What is the scoundrel saying?" demanded Gorman.

Dexter ignored him. "Why do you molest a peaceful expedition?" he questioned.

Parama laughed sneeringly. "A peaceful expedition! Were you a peaceful expedition when you attacked the plantation of Pao Lolita, and murdered that estimable planter? As civil and military commander of this province I arrest you for high crimes. You will be sent back to Manáos for trial."

"Good God!" exclaimed Dexter. "We killed Lolita in self defense after he had stolen part of our luggage."

"If you are innocent you will have an opportunity to prove it. It is my duty to place you all under arrest. If you resist, you will be slain to the last man."

"May I talk with the others?"

"I shall allow you a few moments."

Dexter rapidly informed his companions of the situation.

"We put our heads into the lion's mouth," said Gorman bitterly. "He says he has a machine gun. Do you believe it?"

"It's possible."

"What do you advise?"

"We're trapped. We have got to surrender. He offers sanctuary to Louise if we refuse."

"I won't accept it. I stay with you," cried the girl.

"A machine gun will wipe us out in a few seconds."

"No it won't," exclaimed Gorman. "Tell him to depart and we will hold a conference. In fifteen minutes we'll make our decision."

"Man alive, what can we do?"

"You tell him that."

"In a quarter of an hour," replied Parama, "I shall open fire with the machine gun. I implore you to send the young lady through the lines if you are insane enough to resist."

"We shall try to persuade her to go," replied Dexter. "We seem to be in your power and I shall endeavor to induce the chief, Mr. Gorman, to surrender."

Parama bowed and backed away.

"Listen, all of you," commanded Gorman. "The machine gun can't kill us if it can't hit us. He has nothing out there but a parcel of cowardly Indians and a few equally cowardly Portuguese. Every man take two rifles, and slip down the bank of the river four or five feet. They are on rising ground and they won't get enough depression on their gun. The bank is a ready-made trench. Let them fire a belt of ammunition. Locate the gun, concentrate your fire on it, and when I give the word, charge it. Come on. Louise, you remain here when we make our rush."

The night was so dark that they could see nothing of their enemies, and the darkness was equally favorable to them. The river bank was steep and their camp six or eight feet above the water's edge. They slithered over the edge and lay just below the brink, Louise between Les and Dexter.

"Now, men," commanded Gorman, "empty the magazine of one rifle at the point where the gun is. Disregard any other fire. If we capture the gun we capture the place. When I give the word, grab the loaded rifle. I wish to heaven we had bayonets."

"These niggers won't wait for the bayonet. Sure, this is like old times in the Irish Guards. Boys, we are perfectly safe here as the boss says. Every bullet will fly ten feet over our heads." This was from Scanlon, the old soldier.

The minutes dragged on. It had seemed like half an hour when out of the darkness came a hail: "Surrender?"

"No!" bellowed Les Gorman; and the battle was on.

CHAPTER XV

THE BATTLE AT THE LANDING

ABRUPTLY THERE CAME a rattle, a roar, and the *tat-tat-tat!* of a machine gun, appallingly loud in the still night air of the Rio Negro.

Regardless of bullets, Gorman kept his head above the brink of the bank and his eyes upon the point of fire. The gun was located about a hundred and fifty feet distant, and to the left of Panama's house.

The rattle ceased.

"Concentrate your fire upon a point thirty feet to the left of the house," he commanded. "Let them have it."

It seemed as though one machine gun were replying to another as the party's six magazine rifles poured their leaden contents at the unprotected station of the Brazilian weapon.

Gorman dropped his empty weapon and seized a loaded rifle.

"Come on, boys," he shouted. "Keep close and run like Sam Hill!"

They surged over the bank, Dexter among them; but he hesitated for a second. In that instant Louise clambered over the top and ran after her brother. Dexter, only a couple of feet behind her, overtook her and grasped her arm.

"Go back," he implored.

"Let me alone," she flashed. "You coward!"

The rush of feet was heard and a dropping fire opened from

along a hundred-foot front; but the riflemen were shooting in the dark.

"When the gun opens again, drop flat and wait until it stops," commanded Gorman.

They had covered fifty or sixty feet, when the machine gun spat viciously and the little company fell forward on their faces. The weapon swept the field, but its muzzle was too high—an almost universal fault with unskillful machine gunners—and the targets were invisible.

It stopped, and Gorman sprang to his feet, followed by the others. They raced up the black slope, and Les landed among the machine gunners while they were still reloading. He floored the first man with the butt of his gun in the face. Scanlon dropped the second with a bullet. The others stumbled over the bodies of three of Parama's men put out of action by the volley from the river bank.

"It's an old Maxim," exclaimed Scanlon. "Let me have it. On the ground, the rest av ye."

He jumped into the saddle, swung the muzzle around, fitted the belt, and sprayed the slope from which the Brazilians, unaware of the twist in the situation, were still firing blindly toward the river.

The battle was immediately ended, for the entire army of Dom Manuel Parama scuttled toward the jungle.

"Who's here?" demanded Gorman. "Anybody hurt?"

"Call the roll," suggested Scanlon.

"Dexter?"

"Here," replied Felix. "And so is Louise. I couldn't stop her."

"Schultz, Lawson."

"Here."

"Here, sir," came out of the darkness.

"Anybody hurt?"

Nobody had been hit, which was not remarkable, as the cohorts of Parama were armed with old rifles and had little

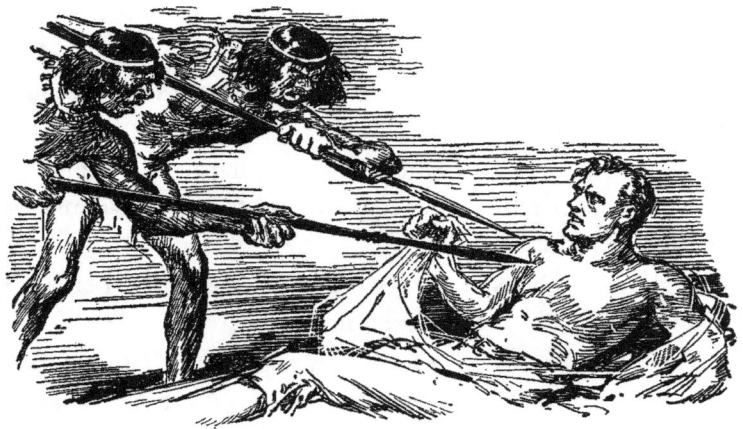

Two ferocious-looking creatures stood over him with spears.

experience in their use, while the machine gunners, it would seem, had never before turned their weapons on an armed enemy.

FIVE MEN had been stationed at the gun, all clothed and therefore not Indians. Investigation proved that three of these were killed, one slightly wounded, and the other only stunned by a blow from Gorman's rifle. The unwounded man was already conscious.

"Tell him to find Parama and order him to come here in person to surrender, or we'll kill all his people and burn the settlement," commanded Gorman.

"Oh, Les, you wouldn't," cried Louise, clasping his arm.

"By God, if they had hurt you I wouldn't have left one of them alive."

Les relayed the instructions, and in five minutes Dom Manuel hailed them nervously out of the night.

"Tell him to come in. We won't hurt him," said Les.

The rubber planter, ridiculous now in his general's uniform, appeared before them.

"You have conquered," he said dramatically. "It does not seem possible that five men could have scattered a hundred. I am abased. I am laid low."

"Tell him to surrender Barnes and we'll leave the place undamaged," Gorman requested.

Felix repeated the question, and the planter, general, and magistrate clasped his hands in the earnestness of his denial of knowledge of the fugitive.

"In the mood he is in he would betray his own mother," said Dexter. "Evidently Barnes did not come here. What now?"

"We'll take possession of the house and hold Parama until morning as a hostage. We'll march him up there. You tell our Indians that we won the battle— What's that?"

The Angoni, who had retreated to the bush at the outbreak of firing, had discovered that their employers were victorious and were out to share in the fruits of the victory. They had secured their weapons from the boats and, shrieking their war cries, were advancing in search of the unfortunate adherents of Dom Manuel.

Fortunately Dexter blundered into their headman, and after a heated argument persuaded him to return to camp or take the consequences.

Meanwhile Dom Manuel had conducted the party to the house, lighted lamps, and with more sincerity than earlier in the evening made them a present of the place and everything in it.

Gorman had all arms and ammunition brought up from the shore and placed in the house, where it would be under his eye, and dawn found the victors sleeping in beds for the first time in weeks, all save Les Gorman, who insisted on sitting up all night in the once beautiful drawing-room while his prisoner, Parama, slumbered serenely in a chair beside him.

As they had anticipated, the capture of the leader had removed all desire for conflict from the minds of his followers. The night passed quietly. Aside from the men at the machine gun only two of Parama's men had been killed and half a dozen wounded, all by the fire from their own gun, which Scanlon had turned on them. During the night they had carried off the wounded to the native huts.

The expedition breakfasted on eggs and farina with Parama sitting at the head of his table. He was as eager to ingratiate himself with the Americans as he had been to capture them the previous night.

"I did but follow my instructions," he explained. "Word had come from Manáos that Senhor Dexter must be captured or, failing in that, must be followed closely until he reached his balata discovery."

"But how could word get here?" marveled Dexter. "We traveled faster than couriers could come. We came from Manáos to Santa Isabel in a sixteen knot yacht."

"There is a radio between Pará and Manáos, *senhor*," replied Parama. "Your purpose has been known since you arrived there. There is a wire from Manáos to Santa Isabel. Indians on the river, short cuts through the jungles, and the drums."

"Ah, the drums," exclaimed Dexter. "I didn't think of that."

"Indian drums informed my natives of the affair at Pao Lolita's. It was my duty as magistrate to apprehend you for that incident. I have done my best. Now I wish you well."

BREAKFAST finished, Dexter conferred with Gorman and Louise.

"I knew that the natives could send simple messages for long distances on their big signal drums," he said grimly. "It seems they can do much more. Of course the drums will report this fracas in every direction."

Gorman grinned. "How about turning back?"

"After this? Impossible. We must manage to cross the Colombian frontier and try to make civilization in that direction." Dexter did not try to hide his concern.

"And the balata?"

"There are only six of us left. We'll be down to two or three by the time we reach the frontier. We must think of saving our lives, not of the balata."

"Well, there is plenty of time to make up our minds about that," Gorman said carelessly. "Now, if Pete were alive, we should have seen or heard of him. Louise, we've done everything we could. We certainly traveled farther down the river than he could have drifted. After what happened last night we have to get out of Brazil as quickly as possible. Pao Lolita might be explained, but here we have resisted the representative of the Brazilian government, and killed several of his men. We'll get short shrift if we should fall into the hands of Brazilians."

"You are going to abandon Pete?"

He laid a hand on her shoulder.

"I believe Pete is dead, my dear. If I thought there were a hundred-to-one chance that he was not, believe me I should stick around."

"We won't survive him long," said Dexter morosely. "But we have to carry on."

Louise sighed. "I suppose you are right. I can't believe that Pete is dead. Maybe he made his way back to our old camp."

"We'll pass it and investigate, I assure you," said Gorman. "Felix, round up our boatmen, and mount that Maxim and all the ammunition you can find on the Irishman's *montería*."

He left the room and Louise, impulsively offered her hand to Dexter.

"Forgive me," she said, "for calling you a coward last night. I was out of my mind, I guess."

"Small wonder. Louise, you were heroic but you were mad to leave the shelter of the bank. I hesitated to make sure that you remained there."

"I realized that afterward." She laughed. "It was the thrill of my life when we charged up that slope under fire. I always wished I had been a man so that I could be a soldier."

"You are a soldier," he said, smiling, "and a brave one. I didn't enjoy that charge. If these people had any nerve they would have wiped us out."

"That may come later. It probably will," she said, suddenly serious. "I'm not falling alive into the hands of Indians or Brazilians. I don't dare ask Les. Promise to shoot me."

He buried his face in his hands and trembled. "Oh, Louise, that's horrible. I couldn't."

"Then I'll have to shoot myself when the time comes," she said without a trace of bravado.

A quarter of an hour later the three *monterías* moved away from the quay and headed up river. Parama stood on the landing and waved farewell.

CHAPTER XVI

A SAVAGE MIGRATION

THE RIVER WAS indescribably beautiful in the first breath of the morning, but Pete Holcomb was not in the least appreciative. By his calculations he had been afloat at least three hours and must have been carried fifteen or eighteen miles below the camp, which meant that it would delay the progress of the expedition a whole day since it would take six or eight hours to row back up to the present camp site. He assumed, of course, that at least one boat would descend after him carrying extra boatmen.

He was carried at least another mile downstream before he had persuaded the *montería* into comparatively still water close to shore, and he drifted slowly another mile before he spied ahead a spot where he dared to land. Retarding his progress by grasping overhanging branches of trees, he edged the clumsy craft to the bank, fastened a line to a rower's bench, and leaped ashore with the rope which he made fast to the trunk of a small tree.

Pete had taken it for granted that the rescue party would be on his heels in a few minutes, but as time passed and there was neither sight nor sound of a *montería* he remembered the obsession of the natives against traveling on the river in the darkness, and realized the problem that pursuit presented.

It did not occur to him that the shots fired in the *montería* would convince his friends that he had been killed by the murderer of the sentry. To him it seemed as if the death grapple in the boat had lasted for hours before the revolver came into play. Dexter had seen him leap into the *montería,* and Gorman and Dexter would surely come after him.

He came to the conclusion that they must have waited until dawn before setting out, which meant that it would be at least an hour or an hour and a half before they put in an appearance. He went back on board his vessel and began to rummage in the luggage compartment in search of food. But he found to his disgust that this boat was loaded only with trade goods.

He settled himself as comfortably as possible in the stern, leaning back upon a sack of cotton cloth. He threw a wary eye upon the branches over his head lest there be a serpent swinging from a tree limb or a hornets' nest suspended within close proximity.

Picking up a roll of mosquito netting lying at hand, he covered himself as well as possible, for legs and arms as well as face were bare, fixed his eyes on the bend in the river around which Les and Louise and Dexter would soon put in an appearance, and waited with reasonable patience.

He had had little sleep the night before, and he was suffering reaction from his experiences. Of course he had acted like a fool in jumping on the boat and he would come in for some criticism from his friends for that, but he had struck the first blow at their enemies, avenged the murder of the poor Brazilian, and rescued the *montería* and its precious contents.

He fell asleep without being aware that he was relaxing his vigilance, and he slept deeply. He was awakened by being kicked viciously in the ribs by a bare foot and he opened his eyes to see two ferocious-looking creatures standing over him, their spears within an inch of his breast.

For a second he supposed they were Gorman's Angoni Indians, and then he realized that these men were bigger, darker in hue, and had streaks of white and yellow paint upon their naked bodies.

Captured by savages—cannibals, perhaps!

Back at camp his friends were discussing his courage, like mourners at a funeral. But at that moment Pete Holcomb almost died of fright.

HE BLINKED up at his captors and felt himself turning green. He realized that the boat was full of Indians and a mob of them were lined up on the bank, grim, terrible.

Bobbing around the *montería* were a dozen dugout canoes, each with a painted warrior in it.

One of the spearmen snarled an incomprehensible phrase at him which Pete took to mean, "Do you give up?"

Pete lifted both hands, palms out, as a token that he was submissive. The spears were lowered and they made signs to him to get out and go ashore. He obeyed with alacrity.

There were fifty or sixty Indians in the band and he observed now that a score of them were women. These were smaller than the men, prominent of breast; and all were dressed in the same costume, a G-string, save for one woman who was young and not bad-looking, who had a couple of yards of blue cotton cloth wound around her hips.

Passing through the savages who regarded him gravely and in silence, he arrived before a very fat man of a deep brown tint who wore around his neck a gold chain from which hung a gold cross. He carried a long stick curiously carved and around his naked waist was suspended a cartridge belt containing a revolver. These Indians wore their hair cut short like white men, and had no ornaments in it like Indians met with down the river. The chief had immense jowls and an undershot jaw. He grinned, probably in amusement at the plight of Mr. Holcomb, and asked him a question in bad Portuguese which, of course, Pete did not understand.

"Americano, me," he replied, pointing to his breast.

"Americano?" repeated the chief in guttural tones. He considered the word and dismissed it as meaningless, turned Pete over to a couple of guards, and ordered the sacks in the *montería* thrown on shore.

As soon as they struck the bank, they were cut open.

With every manifestation of joy the savages pulled out bolts of colored cloth, boxes of beads, knives, saws, hammers, nails, machetes and other items worth many times their weight in gold to the savages.

Immediately there was pandemonium. The squaws fell upon the cotton cloth and set up a shrill squabbling. They tried to tear the stuff from each other's hands until the chief ran among them and began to beat them with his stick while he shouted words which Pete took to mean that everything belonged to him and nobody else.

Unable to resist a look at the loot, his two guards deserted him. Pete glanced at the surrounding jungle and decided to remain with the savages. If they were going to kill him, he thought, they would have done so already. He elbowed his way through the throng which disregarded him and reached the side of the chief.

"*Amico*," he shouted. The Portuguese word for "friend" was one of the few he knew. With a sweep of his hand he included all the treasure.

"Mine," he pantomimed. "For you." He laid his forefinger upon the chief's breast.

"Might as well try to get a little credit," Pete said to himself.

To his delight the savage appeared grateful. He threw an arm over the shoulders of the American who topped him by three inches, and he delivered an address to his followers. Pete interpreted it as a declaration that his good friend the white man who owned all the stuff had made him a present of it and the rest of them must keep their hands off.

The natives drew off, muttering but impressed. The Indian patted Pete on top of the head, apparently taking him under his protection, and then issued orders that sounded like the explosion of a package of Chinese firecrackers. Immediately two men picked up two trade axes and proceeded to punch holes in the bottom of the *montería*. It sank no faster than did Pete's heart.

ALL WAS activity now in the clearing. The stuff was gathered up and apportioned among the various canoes, and the band prepared to take to the water. By signs they made Pete enter a particularly large canoe and the good-looking squaw entered with him. There were four paddlers and finally the chief to complete the equipage. A few minutes later they began to move in single file up the river.

The fleet had proceeded barely a mile when the chief rose and littered a warning cry. Paddles came out of the water. All listened. Pete listened but heard nothing. Not so the Indians. The leader hissed a command, whereupon the canoe headed shoreward and, glided under overhanging tree branches while the dugouts behind followed its example.

Several minutes later Holcomb heard the sound of oars and his eyes gleamed, for he knew what they meant. Gorman was coming down the river. He knew they were invisible from the stream, but when they were passing he would shout at the top of his lungs. The rifles of the white men would quickly dispose of the poorly armed and naked savages.

He was seated forward, the pretty squaw behind him. Whether she read his mind or was just taking precaution, he never knew. A club descended on top of his head and the lights went out.

When he came back to his senses he was lying in the bottom of the boat and the Indian flotilla was out in the stream serenely paddling up the river. His head ached.

After a while he crawled back on a bench and looked reproachfully behind him. The young squaw grinned, and lifted from between her knees a heavy club. Apparently she expected him to applaud her prowess. He returned a feeble grin, whereupon she patted him on the shoulder.

The sun was getting hot and there was no shelter in the canoe as there had been in the *montería*. Pete was not yet tanned, though he no longer suffered from sunburn as he had during the early stages of the journey. He had no head covering and the prospects of sunstroke were excellent. It might be a good thing, he thought morosely. Better die now than be fattened up for a cannibal feast.

Dexter, Pete knew, had informed Louise that he had never encountered a cannibal tribe and doubted whether Brazilian savages actually ate human flesh; but from what he knew of Dexter he thought that Felix had never gone looking for cannibals.

If that was what these people were, they were a merry lot of eaters of human flesh. He heard singing in the dugouts behind them and the paddlers chatted cheerfully among themselves. If he only had saved the revolver he had taken from Barnes! But he had dropped it in the bottom of the *montería*, from which it had been retrieved. The chief wore it now tied by a string to the belt which already contained one revolver.

The light dugouts, each propelled by four paddlers, moved up river much more rapidly than the heavy *monterías* had done and, in mid afternoon, they passed the spot where the Gorman expedition had camped the previous night. It was deserted, of course, but the savages detected signs of occupation. The chief pointed to it, looked back at Holcomb and grinned wickedly.

No doubt all the savages in the Amazon had followed the progress of the expedition with interest. They were too cowardly to attack now, but when the outfit had suffered more losses, no doubt they would join the other enemies of Gorman and Dexter.

His own fate was sealed, but Pete devoted thought to what would become of his friends. They were reduced to six white persons. One of them was a girl; one was Lawson, the companion of Barnes, and probably a traitor; and Dexter, if not a coward, had some yellow in him.

Pete's heart ached for Louise. The best he could hope for was that she would die with her brother—that she should fall into the hands of Aguedarno was too horrible to consider.

AS DARKNESS fell the Indians arrived at an open expanse

of thick grass on the right bank where they made their simple preparations for the night. They had flint and steel and soon had a roaring fire going, and the women busied themselves preparing food. The men, in a body, rushed into the water, splashing and shouting, cooling themselves after the labor of the day. Pete, who had not dared to bathe for days, realized that the multitude of them must terrify fish and reptiles away from the vicinity; so, after a moment's hesitation, he tore off his shirt and trousers and plunged in with them.

The water was cool and refreshing. In two or three minutes he waded ashore, invigorated and for the moment happy. The bath over, the men began to erect rude shelters of branches of trees and palm leaves; and by that time dinner was ready.

The women had been brewing in a stone dish some sort of stew made from peppers and the broad leaves of a plant unknown to Holcomb, and they brought from the dugouts slabs of a bread-like substance hard enough to break teeth if eaten dry. They removed the big platter from the fire and the men fell upon the piles of bread, grabbing a chunk in each hand, and proceeding to sop the stuff in the stew.

Holcomb watched them in profound disgust, yet his stomach demanded nourishment. Finally some one touched his arm. It was the pretty squaw who had well-nigh brained him. She handed him a piece of bread and motioned to him to soak it in the liquid mess.

With a nod of refusal he tried to eat it dry, but could not bite a piece off. Again she urged him toward the platter and he yielded. By this time most of the men had retired and he found a place at the platter. He sopped the bread around, softened it and bit off a mouthful. The stew was fiery with pepper and almost choked him. The warriors howled with laughter as he yielded to a fit of coughing which angered Pete. He succeeded in eating the stuff without further distress.

The women now rushed to the feast, while the men threw themselves on the ground. There was no conversation, no exchange of ideas. Half an hour after the meal the savages had crawled into the shelters and were sound asleep save for half a dozen who stood leaning on their spears at various points about the camp.

No shelter had been offered Pete and he curled up near the fire, which was evidently to be kept going all night. Mosquitoes swarmed and ate their fill of him, for he was quite unprotected. And yet, after considering whether it was possible to steal a dugout and drop down the river, he fell asleep.

At dawn the camp stirred. There was no breakfast, and they were in the canoes and away within ten minutes.

They journeyed up the river in this fashion for ten days. Three hours in the middle of each day were spent at a resting place, but no food was prepared. Sometimes edible fish were caught during the halt, which were thrown into the bottom of a canoe to sizzle in the sun until night, when they were roasted on hot stones and eaten by those who grabbed them first. Pete never got any fish, which was lucky, for after one of these feasts two warriors died of poisoning during the night.

Pete made some progress during the journey by picking up native words from the pretty squaw who sat always behind him in the dugout. He knew that she was the favorite of the chief, but that warrior appeared to have no objections to the language lessons.

HE LEARNED that the tribe was called Tieuchi and that he was part of a migration. This outfit had owned a village and had made some progress in cultivating the soil, but their crops had been entirely destroyed by an invasion of *sauba* ants, which also had eaten all the cloth owned by the women, save the skirt worn by the chieftainess.

After this calamity the medicine man had had revealed to him, by the Devil whom the tribe worshiped, that twenty days' journey up river was a fertile land undisturbed by the voracious ants, and inhabited by an unwarlike tribe that could easily be dispossessed. The band, therefore, had taken to their canoes

and, like the children of Israel, were on their way to the land
of Canaan.

The omens had been good, for upon the second day of their
journey they had captured the white man in the big boat laden
with everything the heart could desire, and they were now
splendidly equipped both for making war and developing the
conquered territory.

There were thirty-two warriors and eighteen women in the
invading army, or rather navy. The disparity between the sexes
was explained by the princess in the most matter-of-fact way.
Before departure they had sacrificed fifteen women too old to
be useful and four old men. Ten men and five women remained
at the old capital to tend about thirty children. When the tribe
had won its new home a party would be sent back to bring up
the remnant of the nation.

Regarding the disposition of himself, Pete's informant was
very vague. His information was acquired over a period of days,
and a large part of it was deduction. At its best the Tieuchi
language was exceedingly limited in scope, and much of it was
expressed by signs which had no meaning for him whatever.

Pete had never seen a North American Indian, but judging
from what he had read about the noble red man he was, men-
tally, several grades above his chocolate-hued cousin of the Rio
Negro.

While Holcomb was a man of city streets and until recently unused to hardship, he possessed a resiliency of spirit superior to that of Lester Gorman, and probably endured the situation in which he found himself more successfully than Les
would have done. Pete was tremendously sorry for himself, of
course, and had little expectation of coming through this experience alive, yet he managed to be amused by the oddities of
the savages.

The same qualities which had made him popular in New
York won the friendship of these bestial humans among whom
he found himself. When a swarm of hornets swarmed from a

tree nest accidentally hit by a paddle and attacked the occupants of a canoe behind, he laughed just as heartily as the chief and his squaw at the spectacle of the Indians diving headfirst into the river within sight of a huge alligator who was so astonished and frightened that he dived in flight instead of taking advantage of his opportunity.

He was almost as naked as the savages after a week and his skin had finally turned brown and toughened. The custom of the Indians of keeping in the shadow of the bank because the current there was less swift had preserved him from sunstroke. And he had been drinking the river water, which was supposed to be full of malaria and typhoid germs, without the slightest ill effects.

He was despondent at times when he realized that his hope of escape was nil and he was doomed either to spend the rest of his life among debased Indians or to be served up in a stew pot when they ran short of food; and then some incident would amuse him madly.

AFTER the first few days no watch was kept on him, for they assumed that he must prefer captivity to risking the wild beasts and serpents of the jungle; but there was always a watch kept upon the boats at night, more to keep off enemies than to prevent him from stealing one and making off down the river. This he was firmly determined to do if an opportunity ever presented itself.

The Indians were good-natured, cheerful and fun-loving, in which he supposed they differed from their red brothers of the North. They obeyed the chief docilely and they feared the witch doctor, who was a wrinkled but erect old savage who wore a necklace of jaguars' teeth which descended to his belly.

Hunger had forced Pete to overcome his repugnance to their unpleasant food. They had taught him to use a paddle and he was no longer a passenger in the big dugout of the chief. After six or eight hours' paddling he arrived at the camping places ready enough to squabble with the other canoemen for a chance at the stew.

He discovered that the Indians were no better acquainted with the country through which they were traveling than himself, and they seemed to have no plan nor to be devoting any consideration to the method by which they would drive out the present occupants of their land of promise.

The witch doctor knew all about that sort of thing, so the chief's wife informed him. Pete doubted that the witch doctor was any better informed than the others, but had only made a random prophecy and hoped that the prowess of the warriors would make it good.

These tiny Brazilian tribes knew the neighborhood in which they sojourned and were utterly ignorant of what lay fifty miles in any direction from their village. As all dialects differed and as they did not possess the universal sign language possessed by the North American Indians, there was no communication between tribes. In fact, the appearance of a member of another tribe was a signal to murder him.

It was consoling that he saw no evidence that they ate human flesh, and from the friendliness of the witch doctor toward him Pete began to believe that he was considered a mascot, and that while he was in their midst everything would go well.

Pete taught the warriors how to use the ax heads which were included in the stuff taken from the *montería*. He showed them how to fit handles to them and how much more easily an ax would bring down a small tree than by hewing at it with a machete.

About the tenth day the princess or queen or squaw—he called her all these things to her face, and she received them with equal aplomb—informed him that the chief expected him to take a prominent part in the battle with the unknown tribe whose domain they were rapidly approaching. There had been a conference between the chief and the witch doctor, and it had been decided to give him one of the revolvers suspended from his majesty's belt, with which he was to slaughter many of their enemies.

There were still four cartridges in the gun he had taken from Barnes, and a box of cartridges in the stuff taken out of the *montería* settled the ammunition problem. It thrilled him to think that he was to get back the firearm. However, Pete had no desire to take part in a massacre of unoffending savages, nor did he wish to risk his skin in a battle between two hordes who were equally abhorrent to him.

It would be a contest of blow-guns and spears, and his flesh crept at thought of a poisoned dart penetrating his body. Nevertheless, it was not politic to show timidity. He boasted to the woman of how many enemies he would kill for them if he were intrusted with the revolver.

It developed that the chief had no cartridges for his weapon, an ancient forty-five, and it was highly probable that it would explode in his hand if he did possess ammunition; but the ruler had no curiosity to fire a gun. He wore it as a badge of office.

Pete eagerly demanded to know when they would give him his weapon, and was disappointed to learn that it would be intrusted to him just before the battle. He argued that he needed it to practice shooting, but they replied that the report of a weapon would alarm their enemies or bring down upon them other savages with whom they did not desire to wage war.

CHAPTER XVII

THE ASSAULT ON
THE STOCKADE

ON THE EIGHTEENTH day they began to move with great caution. The river at that point had narrowed to a little over a quarter of a mile and the current was much more rapid and the banks less thickly wooded. According to Holcomb's calculations they had traveled three hundred and fifty to four hundred miles, and they must be close to the Colombian frontier; in fact, the left bank might now be Colombia. This was the route which Gorman and Louise and Dexter were following, but they could only travel half as fast as the savages in their light dugouts. Even if all had gone well with the expedition, they still must be a hundred and fifty miles south.

On the evening of the nineteenth day the Indians did not land, but made fast their boats to overhanging branches in a thickly wooded spot and lay down to sleep without their dinner.

There was a ludicrous side to the situation. These children of the jungle believed so completely in the revelation of the witch doctor that they took it for granted that they had come directly to a prosperous settlement inhabited by unwarlike natives and that the village which would be their future home was located within a few miles of the spot where they arrived on their nineteenth evening.

At dawn two Indians in a dugout set out alone with instructions to land a few hours up river and discover whether the enemy had any warning of their coming, and if they were preparing for defense. The scouts were not ordered to discover if there were a tribe of prosperous Indians in that vicinity. That was taken for granted.

Pete gave the witch doctor credit for a certain amount of judgment. While the country in which they had arrived was still hot and tropical it was not nearly so humid as the country down river, and the character of the vegetation had changed greatly. It was now more forest than swampy jungle, less dense and presumably more habitable. It was even possible that it was outside the domain of the *sauba* ants.

All day they loafed in the shadow of the bank and late in the afternoon a low shout went up as the dugout of the scouts was spotted in the distance.

The canoe approached rapidly and slid alongside that of the chief who questioned its occupants anxiously.

They had landed two hours up river as ordered, they explained and immediately found traces of inhabitants. The woods were not very thick and the ground was firm and they followed a trail for an hour and had come in sight of the enemy.

These people occupied the biggest *moloca* or big house they had ever seen; it must hold two hundred inhabitants. There was a high stockade around the settlement, and a great area of land where things were growing. The individuals whom they had seen outside the stockade were fat. They had seen fowl and pigs and beautiful women.

The chief's eyes glowed and he shouted congratulations to the witch doctor whose canoe had come alongside.

It seemed to Pete that the medicine man did not look so happy. To his shrewd mind, a powerful village protected by a wall might be too tough a nut for his countrymen to crack, but the simple-minded chief of the tribe had no such qualms. Had not the witch doctor's particular devil made him and his people a present of this place? All the Tieuchi had to do was to shout and the wall would fall down and the inhabitants would then present their breasts to the spear.

The chief gave the word to proceed and the file of canoes

moved cautiously up river, camouflaged perfectly by the over-hanging vegetation.

HOURS passed and night was falling when they arrived at the spot where the scouts had landed. They went ashore, but did not light a fire lest they alarm the enemy, and they munched the hard bread which they dipped into the river water to save their teeth.

Without a fire the Indians dared not sleep on shore, so they returned to their canoes and slept until just before dawn. The chief, Muko, ordered Holcomb to keep close to him, the women were told to follow behind the warriors. Preceded by the scouts, they crept cautiously through the forests whose night cries were not yet silenced by the coming of dawn.

They moved in single file with the witch doctor remaining back with the women. Every man had a blow-gun and a quiver of darts and a spear. No instructions as to the order of battle had been issued as far as Pete Holcomb knew. Evidently they had but one way of fighting; go in anywhere and hit anybody who appeared in front of them.

Peter Holcomb, Class of 1922, Vardon University, moved forward to battle with this mob of ferocious savages in a state of mind that is easily appreciated. He marched because he would get a spear between his shoulder blades if he didn't. In his pocket was a box of cartridges, but as yet he had not received the revolver.

He was unarmed, and shortly two savage tribes would be thrusting, stabbing and throwing poisoned darts on all sides of him. His prospects of surviving, no matter how the battle went, were about one in a thousand, or, in modern slang, a Chinaman's chance.

Gray light penetrated through the jungle forest as they moved along a well defined path. As natives are in bed soon after darkness, and up with the dawn, the enemy camp would be awake and the Tieuchi had no chance of catching them in slumber. They intended, of course, to burst out of the jungle with horrid yells and to be among the villagers, thrusting and hewing, before their victims had time to grasp their arms. Pete thought the stockade might interfere with this primitive strategy, but Chief Muko, most likely, had forgotten all about it.

He shuddered in anticipation of the slaughter which would follow if the Tieuchi got into the village. Women and little children cut to pieces, butchery of the most appalling character would ensue. And if they were beaten off, the victors would give them no quarter and they would slay the unfortunate white man with the rest.

They had been on the march an hour when the scouts came running back and announced that they were almost in the clearing. The chief turned and spread his arms wide, which caused the warriors to scuttle into the bush at left and right. They would burst upon the devoted settlement in a battle line. At least they knew that much.

The chief detached the revolver from his belt and presented it to Holcomb with a grin.

"Firestick. Kill!" he declared. Pete grasped it joyfully, broke it and saw that its cartridges were intact. Muko's eyes widened respectfully as he saw the apparent destruction and reconstruction of the weapon. He had never known that it did that.

A second later he lifted his spear as a signal to advance and crept forward, Pete at his heels.

Five minutes later Muko parted thick ferns and pointed ahead. Pete peered through the opening in the foliage.

A hundred yards distant was a peaceful village. It consisted of a very large *moloca,* or tribal residence, built of boards with a thatched roof, and a number of huts and a small building, the significance of which Pete did not grasp at first. There was an eight-foot, roughly constructed stockade around the *moloca,* but the other structures were unprotected. In the rear were cultivated fields, and between the jungle and the stockade was a garden where brilliant flowers were growing.

The gate of the stockade was wide open, and brown men clad in loincloths, not G-strings, were visible in the garden.

Pete ran his eye over the charming scene and it rested upon the building outside the stockade. It had a rude tower at one side and on top of the tower was a wooden cross.

THIS was a Christian settlement! Serene, industrious and helpless. And he stood behind the veil of the jungle with a mob of human beasts who, in a few moments would be at the horrible work of slaughter.

Muko grasped his arm. "Look," he commanded. "Kill."

Through the doorway of the stockade came an old man wearing the gray robe of the Franciscans. His thick black hair was tonsured.

"Kill," growled Muko, who menaced Pete with his spear.

"Damn you," snarled Pete Holcomb, "I'll kill, all right!"

He lifted the revolver and shot the chief of the Tieuchi through the heart. Muko died instantly, on his ugly face an expression of astonishment, nothing more.

With a warning shout, Pete Holcomb dashed out of the jungle and he was thirty feet away before the Tieuchi realized that their mascot had turned on them and was joining the enemy. He ran like an antelope, and in an agony lest the poisoned darts strike him before he was out of range.

To operate a blow-gun, the savage must come to a full stop, inflate his lungs and insert his arrow. The rage of the Tieuchi prevented the use of that weapon. Bellowing insanely they poured out of the forest and pursued him. Before he was halfway to the stockade he heard a man panting at his back and he knew that the spear was lifted. Stepping to one side he whirled and drove a bullet into the chest of a powerful brute. He fired twice more and dropped two others who were only a little behind.

The people in the garden ran, screaming, for the stockade. In the entrance the priest waited to shoo them in. A queer cracked bell began to ring in the little church tower. The village was now alarmed.

Pete ran like mad and when a spear whizzed by him, followed a zigzag course to affect their aim.

Holcomb reached the stockade door less than four feet ahead of a savage whose spear inevitably would have penetrated his back. His revolver was empty. His feet had been winged by fear, but his strength was spent.

A man appeared suddenly in the entrance with a rifle and fired a heavy charge into the body of the Indian. Pete dived through the door and fell upon his face, and the priest and the rifleman shut it in the faces of three Tieuchi who began to thrust insanely and futilely at the solid planks.

"Welcome, my son," said the priest calmly.

"*Quanti, quanti?*" demanded the rifleman, shaking Holcomb roughly by the shoulder. Pete guessed he meant "How many?"

"Thirty, *trente, tranti,*" he replied, unable to remember the Portuguese word.

Inside the stockade a throng of converts were running about ringing their hands and wailing. Pete, again on his feet, did not see a weapon among them. The man who had saved him was a grizzled, wrinkled Brazilian who had in his hands an ancient Mauser rifle.

Pete grinned at him. "It's up to us," he said with no expectation of being understood. He drew the box of cartridges from his pocket and proceeded to reload his revolver. It was high time.

The Tieuchi, abandoning their profitless beating against the wall with their spears, were climbing upon one another's shoulders, and already one head appeared above the wall while a pair of hands gripped on the edge were visible beside him.

Pete reloaded in haste, lifted his gun carelessly and shot the first invader in the chest as he was halfway over the wall. He fell inside. The Brazilian fired at the head which had followed the pair of hands and Pete drove a bullet between the fellow's eyes.

DISMAYED, the Tieuchi drew off for a conference. Six of their number had already been slain and five of them had fallen to the gun so foolishly intrusted to their white captive.

Amazonian Indians lurk in the bush and shoot their darts from ambush. Rarely have they audacity enough to attack a protected settlement, but the Tieuchi were insane with rage over the loss of their chief and their repulse from a village which their tribal devil had promised to give into their hands.

They withdrew to the jungle and determined to attack again; and the reverse gave them an inspiration. In five minutes they had hewed down a small tree and they bore it into the clearing. The tree had a dense foliage which gave concealment to the Indians and they moved slowly with it toward the door of the stockade. Probably for the first time in Amazonian Indian history, Indians were making use of a battering ram.

Pete observed a bench at either side of the stockade door which would serve excellently as a firing step. He mounted one of them and the Brazilian climbed upon the other.

At least twenty of the Indians were carrying the tree and were buried in its midst while four or five more endeavored to protect the advance with blow-guns. Pete disregarded these because he saw that their darts were falling short, but even his remarkably keen eyes could not detect a savage among the branches of the approaching tree until it was forty feet distant. At that point he got a glimpse of a head and drove a bullet at it.

Holcomb in the old days had practiced shooting with no notion that it might ever save his life. He could hit the bull's-eye of a target with a pistol from a distance of thirty paces forty-eight times out of fifty. He saw about four square inches of an Indian's face, fired, and that Indian was. dead.

The battering ram, however, continued to advance and Pete, regardless of the arrows which were beginning to come close to him, watched for several seconds before he sighted a shoulder into which he promptly placed a half ounce of lead. The Brazilian was firing blindly and by accident struck a savage. Three bodies lay on the ground behind the tree and it was twenty feet away. Holcomb saw lots of heads and arms now, and he dropped three more Tieuchi and had to reload. When he was ready again, the butt of the tree dashed against the gate which quivered on its hinges.

But Pete could see them and was firing down upon their devoted heads. One, two, three, four, five, six. The gun was empty, but six savages had fallen to Holcomb's weapon while the Brazilian bagged two with his rifle. It was too much for primitive nerves. With victory in their very grasp, for another blow would have brought down the gate, the savages dropped the tree and crawled out of the labyrinth of its branches.

Only half a dozen Tieuchi escaped from the tree and Pete had to let them go because he could not reload in time to pot them. The Brazilian had also emptied his rifle and the retreat was effected without further loss.

The jungle had swallowed up the savages, but from it came shrill and furious cries—the women. He could visualize the mad fury of the chief's squaw, the dusky beauty who had begun by flooring him with a club and ended by being his schoolmistress in the Tieuchi tongue.

Out of the thirty savages at least twenty had fallen and those that Pete had hit were dead men. There were groans from under the tree and the priest wished to open the gate to aid the wounded, but the Brazilian prevented him; a wounded savage would not hesitate to kill a ministering angel.

There were half a score of Tieuchi left and eighteen women. Pete, from what he had seen of them, did not think they would make another attack.

It was more likely that they would slaughter the witch doctor whose false prophecy had led the tribe to destruction and then, with two women apiece, either return to the remnant of their tribe hundreds of miles down the river or abandon them and settle in some uninhabited spot nearer at hand.

CHAPTER XVIII

AN UNCONSCIOUS WARNING

HOLCOMB CLIMBED DOWN from his bench and was embarrassed to have the old priest drop on his knees and kiss his hand, an example which was immediately followed by the men, women, and children who had huddled in agony until the issue of the battle was decided.

The Brazilian rifleman waited his turn and then attempted to kiss him. Pete Holcomb might be considered of no importance in New York, but here was a community which considered him its savior.

Well, he was. If Muko, the chief, had not stupidly assumed that the white captive was a loyal follower, there was no doubt that the Tieuchi would have taken the village and have slain the inhabitants. The little mission would have been destroyed and Christianity in that section blotted out.

The priest drove away his followers at last and addressed Holcomb in Portuguese. When Pete shook his head the old man spoke to him in excellent French.

"By what miracle of the Virgin did you come to our aid in our hour of greatest need?" he asked. "You are not Brazilian. Are you French or English?"

"American, *mon père.*"

"Ah, then you are one of the friends that Dom Carlos Aguedarno is expecting."

"Eh, what's that you said, father?"

"Dom Carlos Aguedarno. He is expecting you, is he not?"

"He may be," replied Holcomb, thunderstruck, "but I certainly was not expecting him. Where was he during all the shooting?"

"He is hunting the jaguar. With him are Senhor Tabrano and Senhor Sanchez. You know them?"

"Never heard of them in my life."

"Is that true? Well, my son, the Mission of Santa Maria of Lisbon owes its present existence to God and you. Everything we have is yours."

He conducted Holcomb through the wide door of the great *moloca*. The place was dark, lighted only by the doors at either end. It must have measured eighty feet by one hundred, and was large enough to house a whole tribe, but it was no longer a place of residence, and seemed to be used as a granary.

"When the first father came he found our Indians primitive savages like those whom your valor has just defeated," said the Franciscan. "He converted the tribe and taught them that it was not decent for many men and women to live together in one room. So the good natives built houses for themselves and the *moloca* is now used as a meeting-place in rainy weather and a storehouse for our surplus crops against a famine."

"How long have you reverend gentlemen been here?" asked Holcomb.

"For more than half a century, my son."

They passed out of the *moloca* and Pete discovered that there was no stockade on this side, but scores of small thatched huts. Had the incredibly stupid Tieuchi reconnoitered they would have discovered that the place was defenseless in the rear, but the bull-headed chief had hurled his forces like madmen against a high wall. It was the invitingly open gate which had lured the savages to their destruction.

Pete called attention to this weakness and the priest nodded.

"My predecessor, Father Augustus, intended to enclose the entire settlement with a wall, but he had only time to finish the wall in front before he died. That was two years ago… I am Father Pedro."

"Why didn't you finish it?" Pete asked bluntly.

"Father Augustus lacked faith in the protection of God," he replied. "We came here not to wage war or even to defend ourselves. Had my people weapons they would not have raised them against these savages. Christians are always glad to die, my son."

"Well, it's lucky I had a revolver and that fellow back there had a gun," Pete replied, "or you and your people would have had their wish. There are still a dozen or so of those brutes lurking in the jungle and you had better take some precautions."

"They will not harm us now. As soon as I have taken you to your quarters in my house I am going back to aid those wounded men."

HOW WAS it possible, Pete marveled, that Aguedarno, whom they had left in Manáos wearing a top hat and frock coat, could have arrived in this remote spot, nearly a thousand miles from Manáos by the zigzag river route, ahead of himself and the Gorman expedition?

And had not Les and himself troubles enough without the scoundrel arriving on the scene in person? So Aguedarno had told the old priest that he was expecting American friends. No doubt he was preparing a warm reception for them.

It meant, however, that Louise and Les and Dexter were still alive and moving up river. Aguedarno, damn him, had means of learning whether a catastrophe had befallen the expedition; and if he expected Les and Dexter, it meant that they were still going strong.

It brought a warm glow to Pete's heart to think of seeing Louise again and of grasping the hand of old Les Gorman.

He found bread and coconut milk, and ate and drank. Then he stripped off his rags and donned cotton trousers and a coat which he found hanging on a nail in the inner room. They were a trifle small for him.

In about half an hour Father Pedro returned and smiled to see that his guest had made himself at home and comfortable.

"Tell me how it is possible for Senhor Aguedarno to be in this place?" Pete blurted out.

"I do not know," replied the priest. "He came a few days ago accompanied by Senhor Tabrano and Lieutenant Sanchez. Senhor Tabrano operates a small balata plantation some seventy-five kilometers to the west."

"Aguedarno was in Manáos when I left it many weeks ago and it doesn't seem possible he could be here as soon as this. Will you do something for me, *mon père?* Aguedarno is my enemy. He will kill me if he finds me. Do not let him know that I am here!"

"I cannot lie, young man."

"You owe me something, you know. You wouldn't have a mission and a lot of parishioners if it were not for me."

"It was the Lord's will that our work here should not be ended, my son. Yet I am grateful to you as his instrument. I shall not inform Dom Carlos that you are here and I shall instruct my people to keep silent."

"Thank you, father. It may save my life and the lives of others."

"And now, I am curious," said the priest who seated himself in one of the crude chairs.

He listened intently while Holcomb narrated his experiences and when he had finished the old man crossed himself and mumbled something in Latin.

"My son, I am saying a mass in a little while for the repose of the souls of those who were killed. Would you like to be present?"

"If you don't mind, I would rather not. I'm beginning to feel bad already and the service would make me feel worse."

"That is repentance. I am sure the Lord will forgive you for what you have done, since you repent. Take heart, my son."

A few moments later the cracked bell in the little tower of the church began to toll. The priest raised two fingers of his right hand and made the sign of the cross over Holcomb's head and then left the hut. Pete stepped to the door and saw the inhabitants of the settlement moving toward the sacred edifice. The women wore a garment which hung straight down from neck to knees.

What an opportunity they were offering the remnant of the Tieuchi! No watch, no regard for the savages lurking in the jungle. Pete examined his weapon and hastened through the *moloca* to the stockade. But on one of the firing steps stood the Brazilian rifleman, Juan Juego, with a keen eye on the jungle. He bowed and smiled as the American approached.

THE SUN was broiling hot and since all was quiet Holcomb retreated into the dark *moloca* to ponder over his course of action.

The little settlement was a couple of miles from the river which might have aided Providence to secure its immunity for half a century. Not only the rubber and balata hunters, but the Indians traveled by water and rarely ventured far from the banks of the river. Gorman and his little band, toiling up the river, would pass by without a suspicion that their lost companion was in safety only two miles inland, and they would blunder into whatever trap Aguedarno was laying for them. Obviously his course was to get possession of a canoe and drop down the river until he came upon them. Nor should he delay. Among these Christian Indians there might be a spy. The old rifleman was probably in the employ of Aguedarno.

By his calculations, the Gorman expedition must be a week or ten days' journey down river, and it would be exceedingly dangerous for him to attempt to depart alone while the Tieuchi were still in the vicinity. In a boat, on the river, his revolver would beat them off, but going through the jungle to the river bank he would be at the mercy of spear or blow-gun.

He was reassured by the report of one of the mission Indians that the Tieuchi had returned to their boats with their women, and were paddling downstream. So two days later, accompanied by the entire population of the mission, Pete retraced his steps through the jungle path up which he had marched with the Tieuchi horde. Two Indians stood on the bank holding a small dugout in which had been placed a week's supply of food, which consisted of farina, black bread and dried fish.

As he stepped into the canoe the throng fell upon their knees and called down blessings upon his head while the priest pronounced a benediction upon him. Pete had a fleeting wish that Louise could see what these people thought of him.

The start was made an hour after dawn. Holcomb paddled out into the middle of the river and let the current take him in its grasp, content to use his paddle only to keep her headed directly downstream. He was in no mind to overtake the Tieuchi though he was confident that his revolver was a match for them, and the river would transport him forty miles or more each day. In two or three days he was hopeful of encountering the *monterías* of Lester Gorman.

CHAPTER XIX

OUT OF THE SKY

IT WAS STILL cool on the river and Pete was so happy he broke into song. Never in his life had he felt so perfectly fit. Never had he been so confident of his prowess. He pictured the astonishment and delight of his friends. And Louise! How would she receive him? Was she engaged to Dexter by this time? It was probable.

As the day wore on, the complete loneliness of the river began to get him. Hour after hour on a wide, deep stream with the jungle on either side and never a sight of a living creature if one excepted alligators who occasionally pushed their ugly snouts above water, drew in gulps of air and sank again.

It would be so easy to pass his friends who might be proceeding under the canopy of the bank where the current was slightest. He was a conspicuous figure in the middle of the stream, however, and even if he did not see them, they would see him. Oh, things had broken so well that it was impossible that he would be prevented from rejoining the outfit.

The afternoon waned and he began to think of tying up for the night. He dared not land at any of the occasional inviting spots, lest he again be pounced upon in his sleep by savages, perhaps the vengeful Tieuchi. He must make his boat fast to an aquatic tree and spend the night in it concealed by overhanging branches.

With the strength and deftness of an Indian paddler he shot out of the current and toward the darkening shore. He drove the canoe through the tree branches which dipped almost to the surface of the river and selected a little lagoon after inspecting the limbs of trees overhead to make sure that he had not chosen a location near nests of ants or the hanging places of the gruesome vampire bats.

All seemed clear. He passed his line around the trunk of a tree which came up through four feet of water, and, while there was still a trifle of daylight, he proceeded to dine.

He laid his gun upon a rower's bench, opened the burlap bag in which the priest had wrapped his food supply and proceeded to consume uninteresting fare with the voracity of the half savage that he had become.

The catastrophe happened as he finished his dinner. There was a tremendous commotion below, the canoe was lifted several feet out of the water and overturned, and Pete went headfirst into the river. He touched bottom only four or five feet down, came up, and as his head broke the surface he looked into a gigantic and horrible face within twelve inches of his own.

His terror was so great that he emitted a shrill scream. He was unable to move hand or foot while he waited for the monster to devour him. But the thing blinked at him from a pair of great protruding black eyes, and turned away; part of a gigantic body protruded from the water and then sank from sight.

For a few seconds Pete stood, neck deep, ready to faint from reaction. Then he realized that he had looked into the face of the manatee, or sea cow of the Amazon, a creature which grows to be ten or twelve feet long, eats only herbs on the river bottom, is utterly inoffensive and was probably more frightened than himself. The thing probably had been sleeping on the bottom. It is a mammal, but can remain for hours under water, and it had risen under the canoe and overturned it.

He shook himself out of his trance and remembered that the water was full of other things virulently aggressive. He grasped the canoe, lifted it, emptied out the water and righted it and then with great difficulty eased himself on board. It was already dark and he realized to his horror that his revolver had gone overboard and also his supply of food.

UNARMED, without anything to eat, he was alone in the sinister wilderness. His plight unnerved him. He shook his fist and gibbered curses at the spot where the clumsy beast had vanished and for hours he cowered in the boat in his clammy clothes, shivering and a prey to every terror. Sleep was impossible. The shrill jabber of the jungle hammered on his nervous system. With his clothing moist on his back he knew that he was inviting malaria. Not even the first night of his captivity to the Tieuchi was as dreadful as this one.

Morning came at last and Peter Holcomb, cynic, knelt down in the bottom of the canoe and thanked his God. As the light grew stronger he could see his revolver lying on the bottom, but the fish had completely devoured the packages of food. He could see the slithering fish of the shallows moving about between him and the weapon. Some of these creatures, only one foot long, would not hesitate to attack a man, but the man-eaters might not be among this lot. He saw his paddle entangled in a mess of water lilies a dozen feet distant, its blade within arm's length, and he retrieved it and then gazed wistfully down at his gun.

Eight or nine hours at the bottom of the river hadn't been of benefit to the weapon, and the alleged waterproof cartridges were undoubtedly useless; but if the gun would work, he had more cartridges which had not been damaged by a few minutes of immersion.

The water was clear. Except for the small darting fish, no river denizens seemed to be in the vicinity. He dived overboard, grasped the weapon and then spent ten minutes trying to get back into the canoe with ultimate success. As he drew in his legs he saw an eight-foot alligator slide off the bank thirty feet distant and plunge into the water. Pete was boyish enough to thumb his nose at him.

A man stood with leveled rifle in the cockpit.

He tried the gun and it stuck. Oil would fix it, but he had no oil. He dried it as well as he could in hope of avoiding the complication of rust, sighed and laid it on the bottom of the canoe. The weapon was useless except as a menace, and wild beasts and savages do not understand threats.

With a sigh he pushed out into the stream. It was exceedingly unlikely that he would encounter his friends for two or three days which meant other horrible nights tied up to the river bank, at the mercy of the things of the dark. Yet he dared not float down river in the night lest he pass the encampment of Les Gorman and his party without being aware of it.

He could go without food for two or three days. Back in New York he had supposed that he would starve to death if he missed a meal, but his savage captivity had taught him otherwise. He had been for weeks without cigarettes and no longer craved them.

His mood was very black as he paddled gently in mid-river. Gone was his joyful self-confidence of yesterday. He was the prospective victim of whatever happened to want him.

The noonday sun was beating fiercely upon his devoted head when he became aware of a faint whirring sound, the character of which was inexplicable. It grew louder and more clear, and he stopped paddling and listened in amazement. The thing was impossible, not to be believed, but it certainly sounded like the roar of an aeroplane propeller.

It was a plane, all right, coming up the river; but there was nothing visible in the sky. He looked behind him and saw a black speck flying low but many miles distant. It was coming down river; but how could that be possible?

HE WATCHED as it bore down on him at a hundred miles an hour. It was a big twin-motored machine capable of carrying three or four persons. Where could it be coming from? There was no air mail between Manáos and Bogotá, no passenger plane service such as he had read that there was on the Magdalena River in Colombia, no landing stations, no fueling places.

The plane was a mile back and it was descending. He saw its pontoons clearly. In a few seconds it struck the surface of the river and approached him with the speed of an express train. Its engines had stopped and it was sloping up. He watched it stupidly. The appearance of the seaplane was providential—or was it?

The machine darted by him, and he saw two persons in it. It ran on for several hundred yards, circled, and came back. A man was standing up in the cockpit and was leveling a rifle. He recognized him, Aguedarno!

Of course this explained the astonishing appearance of Aguedarno in the upper Rio Negro, but where had he secured the plane? There were none in Manáos, as Pete was aware from inquiries. However, he would soon have an explanation, for Aguedarno hailed him and ordered him to paddle his canoe alongside.

Under the circumstances there was nothing for him to do but obey. In no respect was his condition improved by the arrival of the plane. He had had ample evidence of the intentions of the rubber king toward himself and his friends, and he would have preferred to risk the perils of the river to falling into the hands of the enemy.

Aguedarno greeted him with a mocking smile.

"Come on board, *senhor,*" he commanded. "Unfortunately I do not recall your name, but I remember perfectly the circumstances of our last meeting."

Pete made no reply as he clambered into the cockpit of the plane.

"Permit me to introduce to you Lieutenant Sanchez of the Navy of Brazil, aviation branch, Senhor—"

"Holcomb," Pete proffered sullenly.

"*Sí, sí,* Senhor Holcomb," said Aguedarno, smiling.

The pilot, a dark, handsome young man with a small mustache and friendly black eyes, thrust out his hand and gave Holcomb a hearty grip.

"You have much audacity, *monsieur,*" he said in French. "I should not care to travel this river alone in a canoe."

Pete grinned back. "Necessity, not courage, *monsieur.*"

"Your companions are still fifty miles down river, *senhor,*" Aguedarno informed him. "Alas, there are only four of them and the lady now."

"No doubt you are perfectly informed," replied Holcomb significantly.

The Brazilian shrugged his shoulders. "I try to keep a friendly watch on them."

"And what do you plan to do with me?"

"You shall be my guest for a while. Lieutenant, if you please, let us return."

The officer started his engines, whose roar made further conversation impossible, and in a couple of minutes Pete had his first view of Amazon landscape from the air. They flew at a height of two thousand feet over a country of a very dark green save for the snaky line of the ink-like river. In fifteen minutes

Pete got a glimpse of the mission settlement and for half an hour after that there was no break in the verdancy of the jungle.

Away to the west he saw the tops of lofty mountains, the Colombian Andes, and very far to the north were other mountains. Presently they crossed a tributary of the Rio Negro and directly ahead there was evidence of some kind of settlement.

"Our destination," shouted Aguedarno. "Welcome to Stalita, *senhor.*"

CHAPTER XX

THE BALATA PLANTATION

THE PLANE BEGAN to descend, and a river appeared, so narrow that it had not been visible until that moment. It proved, however, to be two hundred yards wide, and the pilot skillfully alighted upon it. He ran the plane to the bank where two men were waiting to take its lines.

Aguedarno stepped ashore and Pete followed him. The pilot was at his heels. They moved over a broad path through a forest of trees of a type which Pete had not observed before in his journey.

His captor waved a hand toward them.

"*Mimusops globosa,*" he said. "The balata tree, *senhor.*"

Holcomb inspected the cause of all his troubles with a lack-luster eye. They were big hardwood trees; that was all they signified to him.

After a quarter of an hour they arrived at a clearing in which were a dozen huts, one of them fairly large. Aguedarno moved toward it.

"You will make yourself at home in my poor house," Aguedarno said courteously. "You understand that we live primitively here."

"Compared to what I've been up against during the last few weeks, this strikes me as palatial," replied Holcomb, smiling.

"So? I have heard from the *padre* of your heroic defense of the mission, *senhor.* I am informed that when you shoot, a man

dies. I shall enjoy an exhibition of your skill—but at a target."
His smile was mocking.

They entered the little house and found spread on the table
dried beef, dried fish, yams, and fruit.

"You had traveled farther than we expected," said the Brazilian, "and it is past the hour of luncheon. Be seated, *senhor.*"

Pete did full justice to the rude fare, as did his table companions. To his delight a native brought in coffee and cigarettes
after dinner. The inner man satisfied, Pete's spirits began to rise.
After all, Aguedarno did not seem particularly hostile; and who
knew what the future held in store?

"You were surprised to see me?" questioned the Brazilian.

"You said it, *senhor.*"

"I have come from Manáos with the lieutenant in his airplane. He is here on business of great importance to the state,
and I have seized my opportunity to meet again you and my
good friends Senhores Gorman and Dexter."

"Yes?" said Pete politely.

"It seems that there have been brutal murders in this region
recently, due to the absence of police. Lieutenant Sanchez came
to Manáos on navy business and received instructions from the
government at Rio Janeiro to aid the police authorities. That
explains his presence."

"Then the murderers are in this vicinity?" asked Holcomb
indifferently.

"We expect them shortly, *senhor.*"

It did not need his satiric smile to supply Holcomb with the
necessary enlightenment.

In some way Aguedarno had learned of the killing of Pao
Lolita, and pulled political wires, and had a naval officer with
a seaplane assigned to capture the killers. He proposed to make
use of warrants for the arrest of the Americans to force from
them the location of the balata concession.

"How do you supply the plane with fuel?" Pete asked, to
conceal his furious thoughts.

"Our machine carries fuel for two thousand miles and it is nine hundred from Manáos to this place. The government has sent a supply of petrol to Santa Isabel, which is halfway. The lieutenant will pick it up on his return. Oh, there is plenty of fuel."

"Indeed."

"*Sí, sí.* It is my intention, when there has been found balata in sufficient quantity to make it pay, to establish a regular plane service between the plantations and Manáos. Balata, being so much more valuable than rubber, can be transported by plane at a profit."

"You seem to have all the balata you need right here."

"Oh, no. There are a limited number of trees and until recently they were worked by stupid fellows who supposed it was necessary to cut down a tree to extract the gum. Scientific methods are being used here now by Senhor Tabrano, who happens to be hunting to-day. You will meet him later. In the new fields which are soon to be opened up, there will be none of this appalling waste. No more killing of the goose that lays the golden egg."

PETE knew that the new fields referred to by the oily scoundrel were the property of Felix Dexter, but he affected not to understand the significance of the man's remark.

"We are pretty close to Colombia here, are we not?" he asked.

"It is only across the river. Colombia, Brazil, what matter? This is no man's land."

"What are your plans regarding me, *senhor?*" Pete asked bluntly. "I presume I am a prisoner."

Aguedarno smiled at him about the way a cat smiles at a mouse.

"*Senhor,* as I told you in the presence of your partners in Manáos, I am a business man. Personally I regard you as an agreeable and well bred person, which is more than I can say of Mr. Gorman; and from what I hear, you are an exceptionally brave man. But for you, the good *padre* and his converts would have been slaughtered by savages. I recall pleasantly our conversation in Manáos. I would regret exceedingly if anything happened to you—but in big affairs individuals do not count. Your fate depends upon circumstances, *senhor*. In the meantime consider yourself my guest. No doubt you will be interested in watching the method of extracting balata from the trees."

Pete grinned. The Brazilian reminded him of Pooh-Bah in the "Mikado," a most polite person who, having agreed with Ko-Ko to execute Nanki-Poo in thirty days, said to the condemned one, "Long life to you—till then."

"I'll endeavor to enjoy my visit," he replied.

Luncheon finished, he strolled about the clearing. Aside from the house of the proprietor of the plantation there were a dozen rude shacks, palm-thatched, of course, where halfbreed workers and their families lived. Behind them was a *moloca* about forty feet square in which the Indian laborers resided.

The clearing was several hundred yards in extent and was partly befogged by a vile-smelling smoke, the source of which Holcomb proceeded to run down.

He found at the extreme rear of the open space half a dozen camp fires burning, over which hung big iron kettles. From them an almost overpowering stench was proceeding. It was something like the odor of burning rubber and yet not the same.

Indians were squatting by the fires, keeping them burning brightly, and occasionally stirring the devil's broth in the kettles.

On the ground, a little distance away, rested what seemed at first to be a pile of white bricks. Pete inspected them curiously. They were hard as rock, but they were not stone and he guessed correctly that they were balata in shape for shipment.

Later he learned that the first discoverers of balata cut down the gum tree, gashed it from base to tip with machetes and allowed the juice which comes from the inner bark to ooze out upon broad banana leaves. The stuff is sluggish and it took a week or two for it to drip. The next step was to gather it, leaves and all, and boil it in a kettle. After boiling came straining, and the boiling-and-straining process was repeated six or eight times. Finally the pure juice was poured in a brick mold and left to harden. The result was balata.

It did not take long to exhaust a balata grove by such wasteful methods, but, upon this plantation, an ingenious system of tapping was being followed. The proprietor was content to take only as much sap from each tree as did not endanger the life of the tree, and he was industriously planting young trees so that his balata would give him an enduring income. Aguedarno, so Pete learned, was half-owner of Stalita.

SOMEWHERE within a few hundred miles was the balata concession of Felix Dexter. Since Aguedarno was established so near it, why need he depend upon Dexter to lead him to it?

Holcomb knew the answer to that. The only roads were the rivers, the jungles were almost impenetrable, a hundred miles was the equivalent of a thousand in an open country. Aguedarno needed Dexter.

A Brazilian officer in uniform would make an arrest. Aguedarno had plenty of men and weapons to support the limb of the law, but to send Les and Felix back to Manáos for trial was certainly not his intention. At Manáos was an American consul and radio communication with the world. Gorman has millions for defence, and justice in Brazil was reputed to be venial. If Aguedarno wanted Louise he would eliminate her three friends in this wilderness where their cries would not be heard. And what could Peter Holcomb do to prevent that?

The plane had dragged him here when he had a day's start down the river from the mission. If he did steal a canoe and make another attempt to reach his friends, he would be captured within a few miles.

Of course it was only a guess of his that Aguedarno was the man who had spread the word that the American girl must be captured and brought safely to a certain place; but he thought that the Brazilian's presence here proved it. His hirelings could have dealt with the Gorman party. But Aguedarno wished to deal with Louise in person.

Pete had some wild thoughts of killing Aguedarno before the expedition and the girl fell into his clutches, but he didn't exactly see how it could be done. He thought he could choke the fellow to death with his bare hands and he would have no scruple in doing it, given an opportunity. The gentle, merry youth from New York City had done a lot of killing recently, and he had slain no man who deserved death in such full measure as Aguedarno. The Brazilian, however, was not the man to take chances.

He remembered that the rubber king had stated that there were only four white men left in the expedition. There had been five after the loss of the hotel clerk, Barnes and himself. Who had perished? He hoped that Scanlon survived. If forewarned, the four white men and Louise, with their splendid weapons, might beat off Aguedarno's outfit; but they would have no warning. They would walk into a trap.

He struck his clenched fist into the palm of his left hand. It was galling to know all this and be unable to avert the catastrophe.

The overpowering odor from the kettles drove him back to the headquarters of his enemy and he entered the house to seat himself on a chair hastily built of slabs of wood with a seat-cushion stuffed with straw. Neither Aguedarno nor the army officer was in the vicinity, but there were two halfbreeds outside, apparently on guard duty. Six-shooters hung in holsters from their belts.

His fate was to be cooped up here helpless while those who were dear to him fell into the hands of the enemy.

CHAPTER XXI

INTO THE DANGER ZONE

FOR THREE DAYS after leaving the plantation of Dom Manuel Parama, the Gorman party moved up river without untoward incident. On the evening of the third day the Angoni headman announced that his people would proceed no farther. They had kept their bargain, transported the white men a hundred miles north and they were now in the territory of dangerous and hostile Indians. They wanted their pay and they would build themselves dugouts and depart.

Payment was a serious problem since two-thirds of the party's trade goods had vanished with Holcomb and the *montería*. After they had settled with the Angoni, they would be without means of barter.

The party discussed their prospects around the camp fire.

"I have a small bale of *milreis*," said Gorman. "Useless, I suppose."

"Quite," replied Dexter. "The loss of the stuff in the *montería* has bankrupted us as far as dealing with the natives are concerned. Even if we got in touch with the savages of this region we couldn't hire them."

"Dexter," questioned Gorman, "since it is out of the question to return through Brazil, how many days' journey do you estimate it to the nearest settlement in Colombia where we can replenish?"

"Assuming we have oarsmen, a month."

"Very well. We have three months' supplies for eleven persons

and there are only six of us left. We can't interest the savages
in canned goods and food capsules and I'm not going to give
them arms and ammunition. Therefore we are not going to get
oarsmen."

Dexter nodded.

"Then this is what we must do. We must abandon half our
supplies and two of the *monterías* and we'll carry on with the
third."

"Row it ourselves?" protested Lawson.

Gorman impaled him with a cold glance. "Unless you have
a better suggestion."

"We didn't sign up to do Indians' work," protested the pal of
the late traitor Barnes.

"I suppose you think you ought to be a blasted passenger,"
sneered the Irishman.

"The idea is, Lawson," said Gorman, "that we can't get natives
because we have lost our trade goods. I am going to pull an oar
and so is Mr. Dexter."

"And so am I," declared Louise.

"And we won't carry you as excess baggage," added the chief.
"Now I am abandoning about a thousand dollars' worth of
supplies and two *monterías*. If you prefer, I'll make you a present
of one of them and the supplies and pay you in full. You can
steer the *montería* down the river."

Lawson turned green. "The Angoni would spear me before
I got a mile," he protested. "I'll take an oar since you all are
going to."

"Very sensible of you," sneered Dexter. "How about you,
Dutchy?"

The German grinned. "I got to, ain't I?"

"You're darned right you got to," said Scanlon. "Mr. Gorman,
we can row a few hours in the morning, lay up through the heat
of the day, row a couple of hours in the late afternoon, have
dinner and go on at night when it's cooler. We're not scared of
devils in the river like the damned Indians."

Gorman nodded. "A good suggestion. Now, men we are splendidly armed and have plenty of ammunition and our *montería* is practically a gunboat since we mounted the Maxim on her. I am confident that we are going to win through, but we all have to work like the devil. I'm going to give you fellows, not only your own wages, but the money which the unfortunate men who have been killed would have earned; and in addition to that you will each get a thousand-dollar bonus."

Even Lawson seemed overcome by this munificence. Scanlon recovered first.

"If we didn't get a nickel," he declared, "we'd stick just the same, for what's going to happen to us if we don't, eh, Lawson? A poisoned arrow between our ribs."

IN THE MORNING they dolefully discarded two-thirds of their supplies and presented two *monterías* to the Angoni with permission to take what they wished of the abandoned stuff. The savages loaded it all in the *monterías* and piled on board of them, glad to be relieved of the task of building dugouts; and they departed joyfully before the whites were ready to get under way.

At the suggestion of Louise they constructed a canopy of banana leaves for the rowers, which took an hour, and finally shoved off. Les, Dexter, Scanlon, and Lawson took the oars while Louise and Schultz were to relieve two of them at the end of an hour.

Unaccustomed to operating the sweeps of the big boat, they made hard work of it at first and showed little progress against the current, but after half an hour they caught the knack of it and moved steadily up river.

By nightfall they were so completely exhausted that Dexter who was chosen for the first watch fell asleep on post, fortunately with no evil result. They had abandoned the idea of rowing farther that night.

Day succeeded day and they crept up river at the rate of twenty-five miles a day. Tempers were on edge. Dexter and

Gorman were on the brink of trouble, Louise was unhappy, and the men were surly and silent. Occasionally they sighted an Indian fisherman who upon spying them, immediately paddled to cover. They were in a game country now and they might have potted tapirs, which are very good eating, except that the work at the oars killed ambition.

Gorman, when not rowing, occasionally took a shot at the wicked eyes of an alligator and usually killed the brute. A week passed and another week; then Schultz mysteriously sickened and died in the night. Something had poisoned him, but they did not know what it could have been since they never failed to purify the drinking water with halozone tablets, and they ate the same food as the German.

Only four men left! They now went ashore to cook dinner, but they were too worn out to erect tents, and slept on board the *montería*. They were very near to the breaking-point.

And one day they encountered the remnant of the Tieuchi coming down the river. The savages were almost upon them, creeping along beneath the overhanging tree branches, when Louise discovered them. The Indians were in a bitter mood and with shouts, drove their dugouts toward the lone *montería*, then pulling in their paddles, and allowing the current to carry them toward their enemies, they rose in their canoes and lifted their blow-guns.

A scream from Louise warned the rowers, who dropped oars and made a dive for their rifles, but Scanlon settled the affair single-handed. He leaped into the saddle of the Maxim and opened fire at short range. Two canoes were emptied of their occupants and the others headed at full speed for the middle of the river.

Louise stopped the slaughter by dragging Scanlon from his seat.

"Stop!" she cried. "Don't you see that there are women among them?"

"Sure I do and it was some of the ladies who were working

the blow-guns," he retorted. "What's the difference when they're all snakes?"

"I won't have it!" she exclaimed.

"Let up, Scanlon," commanded Les. "They've had their lesson."

Half a dozen canoes were paddling desperately down stream while two floated overturned. A commotion in the water just ahead suggested that the ferocious things that lived beneath the surface were quarreling for the dead Indians.

"Back to the oars and get out of this," commanded Gorman. The *montería* forged ahead and soon no sound was heard but the creaking of their oarlocks.

Louise was weeping hysterically as she pulled her oar.

"Better them than us, miss," said Scanlon soothingly.

"Oh, I know, but it was so awful," she sobbed.

CAMPING that night, Dexter stated they might be in one of three countries—Colombia, Venezuela, or Brazil.

"The Rio Negro leaves Brazil and forms the boundary of Venezuela and Colombia for some distance," he said, "but this country has not been surveyed and the frontier of Brazil is not marked."

"Why not go through Venezuela instead of Colombia?" asked Gorman.

Dexter laughed. "Venezuela is like the Amazon, only more dreadful. We would have to find our way to the Orinoco and I doubt if we would ever reach the coast. I have been through Colombia, and we reach healthy highlands much sooner. And my concession is located near a tributary of the Negro which ought to open about fifty miles up."

"Then, if we are at the frontier, our high crimes and misdemeanors in Brazil are of no importance."

"Except that the Brazilian balata hunters roam for a hundred miles into Colombia. At the risk of leading them directly to the concession, our best plan is to go through that way. About one hundred miles east we will arrive at a small village called Mendico, where the Colombian government keeps a company of soldiers. From that point it will be hard going, but the climate will be better and we can abandon boats and take to mules."

Dexter sighed. "I presume you are going to turn down my balata proposition?"

"Would you blame me if I did?"

"No-o. I staked everything on it, but I hope I'm a good loser."

Gorman laughed harshly. "You're too good a loser. If the best route to safety is through your concession, we'll have a look at it. I've got to get Louise out of the mess I dragged her into. That's the first consideration. But if your balata trees are numerous enough to make it profitable to carry the initial expense and the cost of operation, we'll consider getting the stuff out by airplane."

"They are! They are!"

"I'll decide that for myself, Felix."

On the third evening after that conversation, the *montería* headed toward an inviting expanse of soft grass which was the first likely camp ground its occupants had seen for hours.

The nose of the boat bumped against the bank. Scanlon leaped ashore with a line and the men at the oars hauled them in wearily and sighed with satisfaction.

"We can put up our tents here!" exclaimed Louise. "Isn't it nice—oh!"

Men with rifles were swarming out of the forest at either side of the clearing. There were a dozen of them and they were supported by a score of natives with spears.

Half a dozen bullets whistled over the heads of the members of the expedition, taken by surprise and without arms in their hands.

"Surrender!" cried a voice in English. "Surrender, or take the consequences."

With leveled weapons the riflemen advanced and Les saw the futility of resistance. He lifted his arms above his head.

"Don't shoot. There is a woman here," he shouted.

A man stepped out of the hostile ranks.

"I am aware of that," he said, "and I have the pleasure of Miss Gorman's acquaintance."

"Aguedarno!" gasped Lester, pale with anger and astonishment.

"Have no fear, Miss Gorman," said Aguedarno. "You are in the hands of friends and admirers."

"Aguedarno," muttered Dexter. "This ends everything. We're through."

THE BRAZILIAN advanced to the river bank and smiled mockingly at Les Gorman.

"We meet again, Senhor Gorman," he declared. "You would have done well to have been more courteous that day in Manáos."

"You go to the devil," growled the man from Nevada. "How did you beat us up here?"

"This is my country, *senhor,* and I know my way about. It will give me great pleasure to entertain you, and your friend Senhor Holcomb is anxiously awaiting your arrival."

"What?" shouted Dexter and Gorman in unison.

"Pete alive?" exclaimed Louise. And then she began to laugh madly, hysterically, uncontrollably. Les took her in his arms and endeavored to soothe her.

"We thought he was dead, *senhor,*" said Dexter. "We lost him weeks ago."

"Senhor Holcomb is safe and well," replied the Brazilian. "Kindly step out of your *montería,* being careful not to touch your weapons. Ah, a machine gun. It is fortunate that we planned our surprise so carefully."

"If I knew you was there," said Scanlon sorrowfully, "there wouldn't be a single one of you alive at this minute."

"No doubt," said Aguedarno. "A wicked weapon in good hands, *senhor.*"

"Pete's alive, Pete's alive, and I thought he was dead," moaned Louise. "Oh, Lester, isn't it wonderful? Isn't God good?"

"Of course, of course," said Lester, but his voice was without conviction.

He had little hope that Aguedarno's intentions were anything but evil.

The Brazilian, smiling suavely, addressed Louise.

"*Senhorita*, I regret that I must ask you to walk through the forest for a little distance. Our camp is pitched at some distance away from the river and there are no conveyances in the wilderness."

She eyed him apprehensively. "What are you going to do to us, now that you have got us in your power?" she demanded.

"Entertain you to the best of our poor ability, *senhorita*. and talk of business with your brother and Senhor Dexter."

"I told you in Manáos I would have no dealing with you," said Les haughtily. "That still goes."

Aguedarno's black eyes flashed. "I think you will find it advisable to change your mind, *senhor*. Let us march."

He led the way through a trail in the jungle, followed by two riflemen. The Americans and their followers came next, and four armed men brought up the rear. They moved in single file and Dexter and Gorman were able to talk to each other.

"It finishes us," replied Dexter, in the depths of despair.

"We're going to pull out," replied Les. "If Pete is there, I'm not giving up hope. He has ideas."

"I don't know why they let him live. Did you see that devil making up to Louise?"

"Hush," warned Les, but Louise, ahead of her brother in line, heard him.

"I'm not afraid of him," she said in a low tone. "I'm counting on Pete. Think of his being alive, Les! Think of seeing him!"

"What's Aguedarno's plan, Felix?" asked Gorman.

"First squeeze the location of the concession out of me and then cut our throats."

Les grinned without mirth. "No sense in telling him then."

"This fiend will torture me," replied Dexter with a quiver in his voice. "We're up against it, Les."

"Bah. Don't give up until it's all over."

"I—I'm sorry for you people," said Dexter mournfully. "We ought to have come to terms with him in Manáos."

"I'd rather be tortured," said Gorman harshly. "Buck up, Felix. You're an American. Don't let that yellow dog see that you are scared."

"Pete is our hope, Felix," said Louise over her shoulder. "We'll be all right."

"He's a prisoner like ourselves," Dexter replied dispiritedly. "Oh, Lord, to wind up like this."

"Shut up," commanded Gorman disgustedly. "If you tell them your location, by heaven, our deal is off."

Under the circumstances this remark was funny, and Dexter's lips parted in a wan smile.

"I'll bear that in mind," he replied.

CHAPTER XXII

PRISONERS

ABRUPTLY THEY CAME upon the banks of a small stream and as the Americans debouched upon it they stared in amazement. Half a dozen dugouts were tied up to the bank and beyond floated a big seaplane.

Aguedarno looked back.

"No doubt you wondered how I arrived at this remote spot ahead of you, Senhor Gorman. I came through the air."

"That's a military machine by its markings," said Gorman.

"*Sí, senhor.* It is of the Brazilian navy."

Dexter grasped Gorman's arm and squeezed it tightly. He was agitated.

"What's the matter?" asked Les.

"This—why—er—nothing."

"If you please, enter the canoes. Take my hand, *senhorita.*"

But Louise ignored his hand and stepped unaided into the first dugout. Dom Carlos scowled and then smiled maliciously.

A few moments later the party was being ferried across the stream and arrived at the opposite bank. Their own *montería* was visible, being rowed up the river.

"What is the name of this stream, Senhor Aguedarno?" asked Dexter.

"The Aguilla, *senhor,*" replied the Brazilian who had entered the canoe with the three Americans.

"I thought so. We are, then, in Colombia."

"What does it matter?" asked the Brazilian.

"Nothing, I suppose."

From the river bank it was a short walk to the little settlement and Dexter was aware of what was going on there before they came into the clearing by the pungent odor from the toiling kettles.

"You have found balata here," he observed.

"*Sí, senhor.* A very good quantity, but nothing to the discovery you have made."

"I have admitted nothing," Felix replied.

"Ah, but you will," retorted Aguedarno significantly.

And Gorman observed that Dexter turned white.

They crossed the clearing toward the huts. There were two men with rifles visible and several natives tending the kettles in the distance. The rest of the population evidently had been conscripted for the ambuscade.

Outside the largest house Aguedarno stopped.

"*Senhorita,*" he said, "my residence and this whole plantation are yours. You will enter the house, please. The men will be quartered elsewhere."

Louise grasped Lester's arm.

"I wish to go with my brother," she exclaimed anxiously. "Please do not separate us."

"I regret that it is necessary. Do not compel me to use force."

"What's the need of this?" demanded Gorman. "What's your game anyway?"

"*Senhor,*" said Aguedarno, "your sister will be treated with the utmost respect, since she is going to become my wife. You gentlemen are prisoners and must go where I wish to send you."

"Marry you? Never!" cried Louise. "I won't go. Don't let them take me, Lester."

The Brazilian uttered a sharp command, and four rifles were leveled at Gorman.

"*Senhorita*," he said softly, "I pray you, do not force me to shoot your brother."

"I'll go," said Louise firmly. "It will be all right, Les. I can take care of myself."

She ran into the house and shut the door violently behind her.

"This is most unfortunate," apologized Aguedarno. "Follow me, please."

He led the way to a smaller house, pushed open the door, and disclosed Pete Holcomb sitting on the floor with his head in his hands.

DESPITE their desperate situation, Gorman uttered a bellow of delight, grasped Pete by the armpits, and dragged him to his feet and hugged him.

"You old scoundrel!" he shouted. "Gosh, Pete, but it's great to see you!"

Pete grinned, but without joy. "I was hoping I wouldn't see you," he replied. "I thought that you fellows would be smart enough to take care of yourselves. Walked right into the trap, I suppose."

"We did, like a lot of dumb brutes," admitted Gorman, releasing him. "Never dreamed of an ambush, and we were nabbed without firing a shot."

"How are you, Felix?" asked Pete. "Tough luck all around. Where is Louise?"

"In the big house," replied Gorman through clenched teeth. "The brute says he is going to marry her, damn him. I'd rather see her dead."

"I suspected that was his game," said Pete. "I've doped out a lot of things since they chucked me in here yesterday. She's all right for the present, Les. He is mad about her. He was engaged to a girl in Manáos—I might as well tell you everything—Rosa da Sousa."

Gorman's face grew scarlet.

"Oh, the swine," he muttered.

"Where's Scanlon? Is he with you?"

"He and Lawson. Guess they quartered them somewhere else," replied Dexter.

"How do you know this?" demanded Lester. "About Rosa, I mean."

"Sit down on the floor. We have no chairs, and we've got all the time in the world. I've been here a week and I usually dine with Aguedarno. He intends to murder me, but he enjoys the pleasure of my company. Night before last he got drunk and spilled the whole scheme. Wanted me to realize how smart he is."

"Go on!"

"He has had spies on us all the way along and knows everything that has happened to us. He told me all about the way you captured the machine gun from Parama's army right after I disappeared. He lopped off one of our men after another. Barnes and Lawson were in his pay. I had the pleasure of killing Barnes."

"Good boy! Go on."

"He wants to marry Louise, first because he has been mad about her since he saw her in Manáos, and second, because she is immensely wealthy."

"She hasn't a cent except what I give her," replied Les.

"She's your heir, isn't she?" asked Pete significantly.

"I see," said Lester slowly.

"He expects to cop Dexter's balata concession and marry an American millionairess. Pretty soft for a dirty little spig, isn't it?"

Les's answer was a growl.

"**LOUISE** is safe right now," Pete went on, "because he thinks he is a lady-killer, and he expects to win her heart with a few days of gentlemanly attentions. In the meantime we three and Scanlon are going to be tried for murder—Pao Lolita and the peons you killed at Parama's."

"You killed Lolita!" exclaimed Dexter.

The other two looked at him. The man was green and his teeth were chattering.

"What did I tell you, Pete?" asked Gorman scornfully.

"Guess you were right, at that. You are a heck of an explorer, Felix. Sure I shot Lolita, but you were an accessory after the fact."

"We're on Colombian territory. He can't try us," protested Dexter wildly.

"He has gone to pieces, hasn't he?" commented Pete coolly. "Les, Aguedarno is here with a Brazilian naval officer temporarily assigned to the police, and he has a roving commission as a magistrate. He'll try us and condemn us. He'll offer Dexter his life in exchange for the location of his concession, and then shoot him anyway. And he will take Louise over to a little mission about fifty miles away, where there is a priest, and marry her. Of course she won't know that you have been shot while she is absent. In that way his wife will inherit the money you made in Nevada."

Dexter had sunk into a corner and was sobbing like a woman.

Pete nodded toward him. "It looks as though Aguedarno would have no trouble finding out where Felix's balata forest is."

Dexter looked up. Tears were streaming down his cheeks. "He has found it," he said, to their astonishment. "This is it. I realized it as soon as we crossed that little river. It's in Colombia, I tell you."

Pete grinned. "That is going to disappoint Aguedarno, because he doesn't think this field is very rich. I'm glad he is in for one disappointment."

"Holcomb," said Gorman gravely, "you are a changed man from the kid I used to know. You are hard and flippant. We're in a horrible predicament. My sister is in terrible clanger, and you used to be fond of her. The poor girl has pinned her hopes on you since she learned that you are alive, foolishly, of course.

Has thinking about what is going to happen to you made you glad that we are going to share your fate and Louise will meet with a worse one?"

Pete laid his hand on his friend's shoulder and lowered his voice.

"No," he whispered. "I've got a scheme."

CHAPTER XXIII

THE GLOVED FIST

WHEN LOUISE ENTERED the house of Aguedarno she found the table laid for dinner for three, which heartened her a little. At least she would not be forced to dine *tête-à-tête* with the scoundrel. A native woman, who was laying knives and forks upon the cotton tablecloth, bobbed her head and smirked when Louise entered, pushed open a door to an inner room and showed the girl a small mirror hanging over a chest of drawers of homemade construction. There was a folding army cot in a corner, a chair, and no other furniture.

As Louise was a woman, her perturbation of mind did not prevent her from gazing in the first mirror she had seen for weeks. Her face was thin and her skin was covered with a deep tan which contrasted strangely and stunningly with her big blue eyes and her corn-colored hair. Just before leaving Manáos she had bobbed it closely, but it had grown out and was at the unruly stage.

She patted it mechanically. Her comb and brush had been left behind in the *montería,* and she had not possessed powder, rouge, or lipstick for ages.

Why bother? She certainly did not want to make herself beautiful for Aguedarno. She smiled at herself, and the smile was radiant. Beautiful! Never in her life had she been as stunning as she was now after many weeks of neglect of her personal appearance. In a dinner gown—

She looked down ruefully at the torn and tattered knickers

and gaiters, lifted her arms and inspected the fringe on the wrists of the man's jacket. She would like Pete to see her in proper raiment after his long absence, but she hoped she would disgust Aguedarno. She knew she wouldn't, though, for she had read the light in his eyes when they fell upon her as she landed from the *montería.*

The front door of the hut opened, and she heard men's voices talking Portuguese. One of them belonged to Aguedarno, but the other was unknown to her.

"*Senhorita,*" called Aguedarno, "at your convenience we shall dine."

"I am ready," she replied. Perhaps she could use the man's infatuation for her to the advantage of her friends. She would try.

"I am sorry," she said as she entered the room, "that I have no dinner clothes."

"*Senhorita,* we are in the wilderness, and even in that costume your beauty is overpowering," he declared. "Permit me to introduce Lieutenant Sanchez of the Navy of the United States of Brazil."

Sanchez brought his heels together with a click and bowed from the waist. Louise appraised him with a lightning glance and her spirits rose. This man was clean-cut, honest, and a gentleman; not of the same breed as Aguedarno.

He wore the uniform of an aviation officer with distinction, and his smile, while admiring, was respectful.

She gave him her sweetest smile and saw the color creep into his olive cheek.

"*Mademoiselle* speaks French, perhaps?" he asked hopefully.

"Very badly, *monsieur.*"

"Ah, you speak it very well, *mademoiselle.*"

"Please sit here, *senhorita,*" said Aguedarno in English. "You there, lieutenant. Dinner is served. You will excuse, Miss Gorman, the crudeness of everything in this jungle."

As he spoke a servant set before him an earthen platter

teeming with cut-up chicken which floated in a succulent stew. Louise realized that she was ravenously hungry and she made no protest as he served her an enormous portion.

Pop! It was the cork from a champagne bottle, and the yellow foamy stuff was poured into a coffee cup by her plate.

"After our fare during the past month or two, this is sublime," she declared.

Aguedarno lifted his cup. "Your health, *senhorita.*"

"To the health of my brother and his friends," she replied shrewdly.

The Brazilian smiled, but not with his eyes.

"To as much health as they deserve," he answered.

Sanchez, who did not understand English, touched cups with Louise and Aguedarno, and they drank.

"**NOW,** Senhor Aguedarno," said the girl, setting down her cup of champagne, "please state what your intentions are toward our party."

"Let us defer explanations and enjoy our dinner," he parried. "You have no idea of the pleasure your company brings to us who are buried in the wilderness."

"Unfortunately I cannot eat unless I know that my friends are faring well."

"I regret that our supply of champagne is so limited that I cannot serve it to them, but they are being fed, *senhorita.*"

"And then what?"

"I do not understand."

"What are you going to do to us? You did not capture us without a purpose."

"That was my duty," he replied. "Lieutenant Sanchez is temporarily of the police, and I am specially commissioned by my government as a magistrate. Your brother and Senhor Dexter have left behind them a trail of crimes against the laws of my country. They have robbed poor planters. They have violated the law against enforced servitude, and they have killed. You, of course, are guiltless; but they are criminals and must stand trial and be punished if found guilty."

"They are not criminals. It is no crime to defend oneself. Three of our men were brutally murdered, Senhor Aguedarno, and I think you know it."

"It was not for aliens traveling through Brazil to avenge their dead. They should have appealed to the law."

"There is no law, and you know it," she said angrily.

Aguedarno touched his breast. "Here is the law, and Lieutenant Sanchez is its enforcement officer."

Louise controlled herself with an effort. "And what is the penalty for our alleged crimes?"

"If they are found guilty, the penalty is death," he replied with a deprecating manner.

"They are not guilty," she cried, "and you know it!"

He motioned to the servant to refill his cup. Louise covered hers with her hand. The food she had eaten was choking her.

"I shall hear the evidence," he said blandly. "You, *senhorita,* are their best advocate. It is possible that I shall find that they were justified in what they did. It depends on you."

"Oh," she exclaimed, for his meaning was clear. "What a scoundrel you are!"

"You are unkind. I am a just man."

"Your purpose is to force them to reveal—" She stopped abruptly.

He smiled. "My interest is that they should be set free, so that we might do business together; but I must depend entirely upon the evidence."

"Won't you accept my statement that they only fired because they were being attacked?" she pleaded.

"Any statement of yours will have great weight with me," replied Aguedarno.

Sanchez interrupted. "Please," he said. "Won't you speak in French, since you both know the language and I have no English?"

"I beg your pardon, lieutenant," replied Louise. "Monsieur Aguedarno has been telling me frightful things: that my brother and my friends have been accused of murder and you represent the police."

Sanchez looked uneasy. "It is true I have warrants for the gentlemen, but of the truth of the accusations I have no knowledge. Since Senhor Aguedarno is a fair-minded man, you may be sure they will be acquitted if they are innocent."

"But is he to be judge and jury?" she questioned anxiously.

"Trial by jury is an English and American institution, *mademoiselle*. We find it cumbersome and frequently unjust."

"A little more wine, *senhorita*. You are overwrought," urged the polite Aguedarno. "Ah, dear young lady, if you knew the power you wield over me you would not be alarmed."

"Very well," she said tartly. "Release us and permit us to go on our way, since I have so much power over you."

He lifted a deprecating palm. "Unfortunately my duty does not permit that."

"Then I wish to retire. Is that my room in there?"

Both men rose from their seats and bowed.

"Good night and pleasant dreams, *senhorita*," said Aguedarno.

Louise glanced at Sanchez, saw sympathy in his dark eyes, meditated an appeal to him, and decided this was not the moment. She left the table, entered her room, and threw herself face downward on the cot.

CHAPTER XXIV

MOCK TRIAL

COURT WAS HELD in the main room of the house of Dom Carlos Aguedarno at ten o'clock next morning. The dining table served as the judge's bench, and Aguedarno, with some regard lor appearances, had donned a black alpaca coat and put on a collar and necktie.

He leaned his chair against the wall and sat with his hands folded upon the edge of the table. At each end of the table stood a man with a rifle. Lieutenant Sanchez occupied a chair on the right side of the room, and beside him sat Louise.

The door opened and the prisoners filed in: Gorman, Dexter, Scanlon and Holcomb, in that order. Lawson did not appear.

"Pete," cried Louise. "Oh, Pete!" She was out of her chair and across the room and her arms were around the neck of the long-lost one and she was raining kisses on his face while tears rolled down her cheeks.

"Lou!" he exclaimed. "It's great to see you! You look marvelous." His arms had mechanically infolded her and he chattered lest he, also, should weep.

"That must stop," shouted Aguedarno, who thumped angrily with his fist upon the table. "*Senhorita*, this is a court room. That man is a prisoner."

"Where have you been, Pete?" demanded Louise, ignoring him. "You don't know how we have missed you. Tell me everything that has happened to you."

Pete reluctantly unclasped her hands from behind his neck and gave her his familiar grin.

"It's a long story, Lou, and I don't think they'll let me tell it now. There, there, dear, don't cry; and don't lose courage, whatever happens."

"Go back to your chair, Lou," said Lester. "Let's get this farce over with as soon as possible."

"Prisoners," commanded the judge, "stand before this table. Enter, Senhor Tabrano, and make the usual formal charges."

Four armed men had entered with the prisoners and behind them stood an incredibly thin, black-bearded person whom Holcomb knew to be the nominal owner of the balata plantation.

Tabrano stepped forward, scowled at the four captives, faced the judge and made a long harangue in Portuguese.

When he had finished Aguedarno gazed with judicial sternness at the quartet.

"The prosecutor accuses you of various crimes," he stated in English. "You slew Senhor Pao Lolita in cold blood, and several of his workmen. You impressed the natives on his plantation into your service, a crime under the laws of Brazil. You were ordered to yield by a magistrate of this Province, Dom Manuel Parama, and you resisted arrest and killed a number of his men."

Dexter lifted his right hand. He had recovered from his nervous collapse of the night before and was calm and self-possessed.

"A moment," he said in Portuguese. "I deny the authority of this court to try us upon any charge."

"Indeed?" sneered Aguedarno. "I can produce my commission as magistrate signed by the President of Brazil."

"You admit that you are a Brazilian judge, and you, lieutenant, are a Brazilian officer. Since that is the case, you have no right to exercise your functions in the territory of the United States of Colombia."

He leaned forward as he pronounced sentence.

Aguedarno's mouth opened and closed, and his olive cheeks darkened with rage.

"Answer my question!" he shouted furiously.

Lieutenant Sanchez rose and stepped to the table.

"The judge will pardon me. This prisoner has made a statement of importance. We are in Brazil, are we not, Dom Carlos?"

"But certainly we are," shouted Aguedarno. "Let the trial proceed."

Sanchez turned to Dexter. "*Senhor*, you say we are in Colombia. What proof have you to substantiate your statement?"

"The frontier of Colombia is between ten and twenty miles east of this river," replied Dexter. "I know, because the territory upon which we stand is shown on official charts both of Brazil and Colombia to be in Colombia, and because the government of Bogotá has granted me the timber concession which you, Senhor Aguedarno, are illegally working."

"*Dios!*" shouted the Brazilian. "So *this* is your balata discovery? This is the forest you peddled about New York, which you sold to Senhor Gorman?"

"This is it," replied Dexter steadily. "You have been stealing my balata."

"Fool!" bellowed Aguedarno. "There are not five thousand trees here. I thought you had found hundreds of thousands."

"There were more than that a year ago. Doubtless you have cut many down."

AGUEDARNO began to laugh, and his laugh had a keen edge of bitter disappointment in it.

"Senhor Gorman," he said, "a fool and his money are soon parted. We have been shipping balata from here for six months."

Sanchez grasped Tabrano by the arm. "You know whether this plantation is in Brazil or Colombia," he declared. "Which?"

Tabrano shrugged. "Suppose we are over the frontier? It is a wilderness, and what is in it belongs to him who finds it."

"*Messieurs les Americains,*" said Sanchez in French, "I regret my part in your apprehension. I have no authority to arrest you. Our government, if it believes you guilty of murder, must make arrangements to have you extradited to Brazil."

"Silence!" thundered Aguedarno. "The trial will proceed."

The lieutenant faced him. "You have no authority, *senhor.*"

Aguedarno waved his arm toward his soldiers. "These rifles are my authority."

"In your places, *messieurs,* I should refuse to answer questions from an illegal court," said the lieutenant, undaunted.

"I'll drive you from the government service," threatened Aguedarno.

"I'll risk that," replied the young officer.

"Eject that man," commanded Aguedarno.

"I go," replied Sanchez. "And I return immediately to Manáos."

"Arrest him! Disarm him!" commanded the judge.

Rifles were leveled. With a shrug, Sanchez drew his revolver from his holster and threw it on the table.

"I am sorry for you, my friends," he said. "And for you, *mademoiselle.*" He departed between two soldiers.

"You stand accused," stated Aguedarno to the prisoners. "Answer,"

"Go to the devil," replied Gorman contemptuously.

"Fortunately," said Aguedarno, "I have a witness to your crimes, one of your own men who has turned State's evidence. Bring in Lawson."

"The scut, the dirty—" growled Scanlon.

"Silence," roared the judge.

The door opened and Lawson, the renegade American, entered, threw a shifty glance around, and observed with satisfaction that his former companions were powerless to harm him.

"Lawson," said Aguedarno, "did you see these men kill Senhor Pao Lolita?"

Lawson nodded.

"And you were present when they attacked the forces of Dom Manuel Parama and slaughtered several of his men?"

"Yes, sir."

"Enough. I find the prisoners guilty as charged. I sentence them to be executed in the morning. Take them away."

"No, no," cried Louise. "You can't do a horrible thing like that. I implore you, *senhor*—" She threw herself upon her knees in front of the table, shaking with horror.

LES PLACED his hands under her shoulders and lifted her to her feet.

"Don't abase yourself to the brute," he pleaded. "For our sake, Lou, be brave. You can't influence that dog."

"Lou," said Pete in a low tone. "Fourth down, five yards to go, ten seconds to play and the pigskin zooms over the chalk for the touchdown for Vardon. Buck up."

"Speak English," commanded Aguedarno. "What gibberish is that?"

Louise bucked up. "Really, Pete?" she gasped.

"A trick delayed forward and we'll go over the line for seven points."

"Silence! Take them away," commanded Aguedarno. "*Senhorita,* go to your room."

Louise threw her arms around her brother's neck, then gave her right hand to Dexter and her left to Pete, and threw a sympathetic smile at Scanlon.

"Good-by, boys," she said in a voice which trembled. "God bless you and save you."

She went to the door of her room and looked over her shoulder at Aguedarno. "You bloodthirsty beast!" she spat at him.

"You will regret those words, *senhorita,*" he replied, but she had closed the door.

The riflemen began to shove the four condemned persons toward the door when the Irishman pushed away the half breed who was guarding him and stepped into the middle of the room.

"Judge, darlin'," he said softly, "I'm nothing but a hired man like Lawson here. Sure I didn't kill anybody, being a very peaceable person. Ye wouldn't be executing me, now, would ye?"

He extended his arms appealingly and edged closer to the table.

Aguedarno grinned at him maliciously. "You share the fate of the others," he declared.

"Well, now, is it hanging or shooting you're considering, judge?" he inquired. He had reached the table.

"Which would the *senhor* prefer?" asked Aguedarno, sneeringly amused.

Down came Scanlon's hand upon the revolver which Sanchez had laid upon the table. He whirled, his eyes gleaming with hate, and pointed the gun at Lawson who stood at his right and only four feet distant.

"You snake in the grass," he rasped as he pulled the trigger. Two shots rang out simultaneously, for one of the guards had divined his purpose and leveled his rifle. Lawson uttered a strangled scream, for the bullet had passed through his throat. Scanlon died instantly from a heavy rifle bullet which entered his heart.

Aguedarno, snarling like a jaguar, whipped out his revolver and fired six bullets into the dead body of the Irishman who knew how to punish traitors.

Louise had opened her door and stood upon the threshold, eyes dilated with horror. She grasped the door frame to steady herself. Looking up from his ghoulish pastime, Aguedarno met her eye.

"Self-defense," he grated. "The scoundrel was going to murder me, *senhorita*."

She crossed the room and knelt beside the body of Scanlon, and she saw that there was a smile on his dead face. She rose and gazed with loathing at Aguedarno.

"What a pity he did not kill you!" she said bitterly and then she went back into her chamber.

"**THERE** was a man!" stated Les solemnly, when they were back in their jail. "Pete, I had planned to make him rich if we ever got out of this."

"It was an insane thing to do," said Dexter mournfully.

"I wish it had occurred to me," replied Les. "I would be satisfied to die if I got one shot at Aguedarno, and I might not have missed."

"He was my buddy," said Pete sadly. "Well, it was horrible, but in a way it was a good thing."

Dexter regarded him sharply. "What do you mean?"

"He went out quickly," replied Pete, "and it's all over for him."

"Oh, yes, of course. Have you any doubt that Aguedarno will kill us?"

"It's a cinch," replied Pete cheerfully. "He has to get us out of the way. I told you last night about his plans for Louise. He can't have us alive to report this outrage."

"I love Louise. It kills me to think of it," groaned Dexter. "Les, Sanchez may help us."

"I love Louise myself," said Pete quietly. "I have been insane about her since the first day I saw her, but there is no sense in raving. We're not dead yet. As for Sanchez, do you think Aguedarno will permit him to go back and tell the government what a villain he is? That square young officer will never return to Manáos if Dom Carlos has his way."

"What are we going to do?" asked Dexter miserably.

"Behave like men," replied Gorman scornfully. "Felix, you were a fool to blurt out that this was your concession. Now he doesn't need you any more. As for its being in Colombia, he will have all the balata in the place shipped into Brazil before Colombia discovers that he ever was here.

"Another matter," said Gorman. "Dexter, you assured me that there were between twenty-five thousand and fifty thousand trees. Aguedarno said five thousand."

"What does it matter?" replied Dexter wearily. "He lied."

"No," said Pete. "I was watching him and he was so disappointed to learn that this was your concession that he couldn't have been lying. Besides he told me the other day that, while this was the biggest discovery yet made, it wasn't big enough to justify an airplane freight service."

"Oh, he thought of that, did he?" asked Gorman. "He's an able business man if he is a scoundrel. Pete, whatever we're going to do must be done quickly. Think of Louise."

"We've got to wait till night," replied Holcomb.

CHAPTER XXV

TREACHERY?

A GENTLE TAP sounded upon the door of the room in which Louise Gorman was trying to hold herself together by the thin thread of hope held out by Pete Holcomb in his cryptic football jargon. She translated it to mean that their team, stopped in its tracks with a few seconds to play, might win by an unexpected play. What he meant was a mystery, but she had watched Pete from the moment of his entrance and he was by no means as despondent as Les and Dexter.

It was strange that the soft, easy-going, frivolous-minded boy whom Les had treated with contemptuous tolerance, at whom Felix Dexter had sneered, and whom she had liked, but tremendously underestimated, should be the most resourceful member of the party in this emergency. Of course they had accepted Pete's own estimate of himself, taking too seriously his outspoken distaste for adventure and peril; but she had long ago revised her opinion of him and so had Les and Felix. It was amazing how Felix had shrunk in her esteem and Pete had risen, since they left Manáos.

"*Senhorita*," said Aguedarno, when she failed to respond to his knock. "A word with you, if you please."

"I never want to see or talk to you again!" she cried fiercely.

He pushed open the door. "If the life of your brother interests you, you will talk with me," he said significantly.

"Don't come in here. I'll come out," she answered hastily. "What do you wish to say?"

Aguedarno led her to a chair in the recent court room and seated himself facing her. His manner was respectful.

"I do not wish you to judge me by what transpired here so recently," he said by way of a beginning. "You called me a scoundrel and other harsh names. I forgive you because you do not know the facts."

"Then perhaps you'll state the facts," she replied coldly.

"In the first place I was forced to hold this court."

"Indeed? I thought you insisted despite the fact that we are in Colombia and the lieutenant refused to countenance an illegal trial."

"You do not understand. It was my intention to acquit your brother and his friends."

She met his eye squarely. "I do not believe you," she said flatly.

"I am alone, here," he replied, "surrounded by Tabrano and his men who are without principle. I was forced to condemn your party cause of the statement of Senhor Dexter. This is the plantation of Tabrano. Dexter has the concession for it from the Colombian government. Tabrano would not permit him or his friends to depart because they would return and dispossess him."

"So you sentenced my brother to death to oblige this Tabrano, Very kind and brave of you," she sneered.

"They are not dead yet and they need not die," he replied. "Let Dexter sell the concession to your brother. Under the circumstances he will sell it for a *milreis,* and all will be well."

"How, pray?"

"I shall explain. *Senhorita,* I am still a young man and considered handsome. In Manáos is a beautiful young lady who loves me to distraction. You know her, the Senhorita Rosa da Sousa."

"Rosa!" she exclaimed. "Why, she—what has this to do with the situation?"

"From the moment I first saw you I loved Rosa no longer. I was the captive of your lovely blue eyes—"

"Stop that. I'm talking about my brother," she said angrily.

"**YOU MUST** listen to me for his sake," he said eagerly. "You must realize the depth of my affection when I leave everything and follow you into the most remote recesses of Amazona."

"You came here after that balata concession," she said sharply. "Cut out that line, if you please."

"I do not understand what you mean by 'line,' *senhorita*, My English is not what it should be."

"Well, I don't like your lying talk."

"*Senhorita*, not far away from here is a mission and a priest who will marry us—"

She leaped to her feet. "How dare you talk to me of marriage? You, who are going to murder my brother and his friends!" she cried hotly.

"Because when you are my wife, the safety of your brother shall be my sacred charge,"

"Oh!" she exclaimed. "The grand old situation of melodrama. 'Marry me or your brother shall die.' Change the record, Aguedarno."

"Have you a heart of stone?" he said reproachfully. "Would you not make a sacrifice for your brother?"

She hesitated. "Yes, if it would do any good. But you are as crooked as a mule's hind leg. You propose to marry me and you'll execute my brother just the same. That's why you want him to own the balata concession so that you may inherit it."

"*Senhorita!*" he exclaimed, apparently shocked.

"I'm not marrying you," she cried wrathfully. "I'm going to kill myself if Les loses his life. I couldn't live without him and—and his friends, and I'm not going to talk to you any more."

Aguedarno grasped her wrists firmly and brought his face so close that his beady eyes almost fascinated her.

"You will marry me whether you wish it or not, and afterwards you will love me! Women always love me, but you are the only one for whom I care."

"You hate yourself, don't you?" she sneered. "I'd shoot myself and you before I'd let you near, you snake!"

"In the morning the priest from the mission will arrive. When you see your brother and his friends stand before a wall with a file of riflemen aiming their weapons at their breasts your cruel heart may be touched," he said savagely.

Louise hesitated.

"I don't think marrying you would save them," she said slowly. "Look here: I will make a bargain with you. If you convey us all safely back to Manáos and let them go free, I will accept your disgusting proposition—but I warn you I'll make you a horrible wife."

"They will be released before your eyes and placed in their *montería* with sufficient provisions and weapons so that they may go down the river in safety."

"And you'll shoot them in the back as soon as they are out of my sight," she retorted. "No, Mister Aguedarno, If you want me you'll have to take me on my terms."

"That remains to be seen," said Aguedarno meaningfully. "For the moment, I shall leave you, *senhorita*."

CHAPTER XXVI

BALATA INTRIGUE

THE THREE PRISONERS lay on the floor of their hut. Outside two men leaned on rifles and smoked cigarettes made of a foul-smelling plant which grew in the vicinity. Outside another hut a few yards distant a third guard stood at the door of the prison of the gallant Lieutenant Sanchez.

"You said you had a scheme, Pete," said Gorman. "Tell us. Is there any earthly chance for Louise and ourselves? You wouldn't talk last night."

"Frankly," replied Holcomb, "I didn't dare say anything because of the condition of Felix. He couldn't be trusted, to put it plainly."

"I am heartily ashamed of myself, Pete," replied Dexter. "The strain of the last six weeks had broken me down. But I have pulled myself together. If you have any hope, don't keep it from us."

"Well," said Holcomb, "I had the run of this place for a week. They only chucked me in here and put a guard on me a couple of days before you were nabbed. I knew that they would capture you, and if they didn't shoot you out of hand, there was a possibility of getting away. The only reason you were not shot down at the *montería* was because of the presence of Sanchez who wouldn't stand for a massacre of prisoners. I came to be good friends with Sanchez. Unfortunately, Felix, your outburst in court upset things. Sanchez is now in as bad plight as we are.

Aguedarno will never let him go back to report the way justice is done up here. And it also riled Tabrano."

"Tabrano?" exclaimed Les. "That's the prosecutor. Do you mean to say he is on our side?"

"There is a curious situation here," said Pete. "Tabrano owned a rubber plantation a couple of hundred miles down the river and one of his men came across this forest of bully-trees about six months ago. He moved up here with his halfbreeds and natives and started to get out the balata. He sent his first shipment down the river and the next thing he knew five or six well armed ruffians arrived with orders from Aguedarno to take fifty per cent for the big boss. He had to agree because Aguedarno could rob all his boatmen and he would never make a nickel out of his discovery.

"The arrival of Aguedarno with Sanchez in the seaplane struck Tabrano as a heaven-sent opportunity, but he lacked the courage to take advantage of it. There are eight Tabrano men here who have rifles or revolvers, and six of Aguedarno's men. The natives don't count. But Tabrano can't depend upon his own men who are terrified of Dom Carlos. Aguedarno is the bogey-man of the whole Amazon region.

"I got chummy with Tabrano, and he informed me that I would be shot as soon as Aguedarno had captured you fellows because the old boy didn't want any of us around to help Louise. He proposes to marry her, inherit your money, Les, and—well, I told you that yesterday. Tabrano thought, under the circumstances, that it would be a good idea if I assassinated Aguedarno. He promised to pay me well and let me escape. As soon as the deed was done his gang would massacre Aguedarno's bullies and he would own the whole balata works again."

"But you didn't agree!" exclaimed Les. "You couldn't murder anybody in cold blood."

Pete laughed grimly. "I've done only too much killing since I saw you last. I would no more hesitate to plug Dom Carlos than I would an alligator. I said I would do the job for Tabrano, simply to protect the young lady. If you were captured, my price for assassination was your release and that of Louise. Well, he was to arrange my opportunity, but I saw him stiffen up when Felix came out with his claim of ownership. Tabrano would rather share the balata find with Aguedarno than to have you notify Colombia and send the Colombian army to chase him out."

"Oh, damn!" groaned Dexter. "I thought our only hope was to prove to them all that we were in Colombia and not in Brazil."

"**A LOT** they care," scoffed Holcomb. "Now it's possible that Tabrano has decided that it is to his best interests to let us all be wiped out; but he is going to have a conference with me to-night after dark."

"Where? Here?" asked Gorman eagerly.

"No. At his place."

"How are you going to get there?"

Pete laughed. "I was locked up here for two days and I had to keep busy. I swiped a knife last time I dined with Aguedarno—oh, we were very chummy until you people drew near. I amused him, I guess. Look."

He drew a small steel dinner knife from his pocket. Going to a corner of the room, he dug at the earthen floor, a moment later he lifted a section eighteen inches square and disclosed a hole. A slab of wood over which he had plastered a foot of clay had concealed the opening.

"In this way I can crawl out under the wall," he explained and replaced the cover.

"How did you conceal the earth you excavated?" asked Gorman, whose eyes were gleaming.

"Spread it all over the floor and trampled it down."

"Does Tabrano know about this tunnel?"

"Nobody knows."

"Then we'll creep out and attack the guards when it's dark," said Gorman. "I crave action."

"Wait till I see Tabrano," objected Pete. "That's a last resort proposition and I may have a better one."

Gorman gazed at him with admiration. "If we do get out of here, Pete," he said in heartfelt tones, "it will be due to your genius and nothing else."

"Oh, our toes may all be turned up to-morrow. I've been through so much that death wouldn't scare me. But I lose my nerve when I think of Louise."

"That's what turns my blood to water," confessed Les.

"I've got to make terms with Tabrano," said Pete. "Dexter, will you turn over your concession to him in exchange for our release?"

"Of course. I know now that we could never work it," he said. "What an optimistic ass I was!"

"You certainly were," declared Gorman dourly.

"I don't know how the cat is going to jump," said Pete frankly. "If I could talk English to the brute my arguments would be more effective, but our conversation has been in bad French, horrible Portuguese, and pantomime. If we turn over our rights to him with our compliments and eliminate Aguedarno for him, he may be satisfied to let us go—or he may double cross us."

Gorman groaned. "While we are penned up here, how do we know what is happening to Louise?"

"I think she is all right for the time being," Pete said soothingly. "You see, in Aguedarno's mind she has already inherited your fortune, Les, and he expects to marry her; therefore he will try respectful tactics at first. Probably promise to release us if she consents. As soon as he got her away, of course, he'd have us scragged."

During a long, hot, wearisome day the condemned men discussed their situation over and over and over. A platter of farina and a jug of water was placed in their quarters at midday and the same menu was offered them for dinner.

Shadows entered through the one window of the hut, a

square hole near the ceiling, and finally it grew so dark that they could not distinguish their faces. An hour dragged by.

"Might as well go now as any time," said Pete. "I'll be back as soon as I can. Shake, Les. Give me your hand, Felix."

"Pete," Les answered in a voice which was tense with emotion, "if anything goes wrong so that you should not get back, I want you to know that I consider you the best friend I ever had and the finest fellow I ever knew."

"That goes for me, Pete," asserted Dexter.

HOURS passed in the dark hut. They heard watchmen outside talking occasionally and from the native quarters came faintly the sound of some barbaric chant. There was no excitement such as might have been expected if the prisoner had been discovered to be at large, and no shot rang out on the night air.

Two and a half hours passed before they heard a scraping and scuffling in the corner of the room. Both men crept to the hole and pulled Pete through.

"Well?" they asked in agonized unison.

"Sorry I was so long," said Pete. "Aguedarno was having dinner with Tabrano and I had to lie around outside until he was good and ready to leave. I saw Tabrano, all right, and learned the dirt. Louise made things pretty hot for the scoundrel and he had to drop his mask and tell her that he would go through with the execution unless she married him. She turned him down cold."

"Good for her!" exclaimed Les.

"So he is leaving her alone until morning when he expects the priest from the Franciscan mission. The idea is to line us up for execution and take Louise out and show her the pretty tableau. He figures she will weaken, and the knot will be tied at once. They will march us back to this hut, Aguedarno will then take his bride to Manáos in Sanchez's airplane which he knows how to operate, and Tabrano will oblige him by murdering us and poor Sanchez. That's the program."

His companions heard him in anguished silence.

"There is no way out for Louise," said Gorman presently, "If she refuses he will shoot us out of hand and then she is in his power. What kind of priest is this who will marry them?"

"He comes more nearly to being a saint than any human being I have ever met," replied Pete. "But what can he do? If he doesn't marry them, Louise is in what the *padre* will consider a worse predicament."

"But I thought you had a plan which would save us," complained Dexter. "We'll be murdered either way and Louise left at the mercy of that monster."

"Dexter," said Holcomb bluntly, "you've cracked. I don't blame you; a couple of months ago I would have gone balmy in any of the jams I've been in lately. I'm afraid to confide in you. All I will say is that there is a plan, but its chance of success is about one to a hundred. If I told you what it was, you might inadvertently betray it. All I ask you is to brace up and, when you face the firing squad, don't give up hope."

"But why wait till then?" he protested. "How can anything happen then?"

"I've told you that Louise will agree to marry the man and we will be taken back to the hut."

"I don't want her to marry him. I love her!" whined Dexter.

"Shut up, you coward!" said Gorman harshly.

"I happen to love her myself," declared Holcomb. "I don't think she will marry Aguedarno and I hope we won't be shot. Let's try to get some sleep. I need it."

"Another word out of you, Dexter, and I'll save the executioner a job," growled Gorman. "Your folly got us all into this, and the least you can do is take what comes like a gentleman."

Dexter relapsed into shamed silence and all was quiet in the hut.

CHAPTER XXVII

THE PLACE OF EXECUTION

TWO HOURS AFTER dawn the door of the hut was thrust open and a harsh voice ordered the inmates to emerge. Holcomb was lying on the floor sleeping like a child. Gorman sat close by, watching the smooth young face of his friend and marveling at his ability to slumber on what was probably the last night of his life.

Dexter had not slept all night and sat in the opposite corner of the room with his face buried in his hands. He had attempted to speak on several occasions since it became light, but Gorman pointed to the sleeping man and frowned him into silence.

He touched Pete on the shoulder now and the young man wakened instantly. "The zero hour, eh?" Pete said cheerfully. "Well, let's be on our way."

Gorman led the way through the door and stood on the grass at the threshold.

Five men stood in an irregular line confronting him. They were ragged, unshorn, and villainous-looking specimens, each with a bandolier over his shoulder and one of the new Savage rifles, which had been taken from Gorman's *montería,* in his hands.

The little village was awake. A mob of natives had assembled a hundred yards distant in front of a long, low shanty used as a storehouse. One of the riflemen motioned to the prisoners to proceed in that direction. Dexter's knees began to shake and the watchful Holcomb reached out a supporting hand.

"Keep your nerve," he whispered. "They're going to use blank cartridges, Felix."

"Eh? Is that it?" gasped Dexter. He revived like a groggy prize fighter after a shot of oxygen, and marched to the place of execution as steadily as his companions.

The storehouse was windowless and it was evident that the plan was to line the condemned up against the wall. Pete cast a glance around for Louise and Aguedarno, but neither were visible. He saw Tabrano standing just beyond the throng with two or three armed men close beside him. Tabrano made no sign.

"Is it all off?" whispered Gorman.

"No—at least I hope not."

The soldiers of the jungle behind them prodded them with the muzzles of their rifles toward the wall of the storehouse and they lined up side by side. A native came from somewhere bearing pieces of rope for the purpose of binding their arms behind their backs, but as he approached the prisoners Tabrano stepped forward and waved the man away.

"It is not necessary," he said sharply. "These are brave gentlemen."

A gasping sigh came from the throat of Peter Holcomb.

"Put your hands behind your backs," he said in a low tone. "Do what I say, Dexter."

The five men who had escorted them to the place of execution now took up a position less than thirty feet distant and a great chattering came from the mob of native workmen.

"What are we waiting for?" cried Dexter hysterically in Portuguese.

"For Dom Carlos Aguedarno," replied Tabrano. "He is in command here."

There were five minutes of agonizing inaction and then they

saw Aguedarno approaching, followed by Louise and a man in a gray robe, the priest from the mission.

"Oh, the dog, to bring her here!" muttered Gorman. "If I could get my hands around his neck—"

"Shut up, it's his game, as I told you," hissed Pete between clenched teeth.

The trio came rapidly upon the scene and Louise tried to rush forward, but was grasped by the Brazilian and held tightly in his arms. The priest continued to approach.

"May I give you the consolation of religion?" he asked pitifully. "Monsieur Holcomb, it touches my heart to see you here. I have pleaded with Dom Carlos, but he has a heart of stone."

"We are not Catholics and we do not need a priest," said Holcomb curtly. "Go back, father, and get out of the line of fire."

The priest lifted his hand in sad benediction and moved away, his face working with emotion.

LOUISE and Aguedarno were in passionate altercation and the girl was screaming, "No, no, no!"

"Louise," shouted Lester, "I forbid you to agree to any proposition of that coyote."

Aguedarno shouted to natives standing by who rushed forward and two of them seized the girl by the arms and dragged her away from the Brazilian.

"You have had your chance," he said to her loudly in English. "Now I must do my duty."

He walked swiftly to the firing squad who slouched with their rifles resting on the ground and began to give them their instructions. Louise broke from the natives and rushed forward, screaming wildly. The Indians pursued her and captured her and dragged her out of the line of fire.

"Make ready," commanded Aguedarno. The riflemen leisurely lifted their rifles.

Pete Holcomb's right hand came from behind his back and

in it was a revolver which immediately spat fire. One, two, three, four, five, six bullets tore out of the moving muzzle of the weapon.

Like a row of ninepins struck by a ball, the firing squad toppled over. Aguedarno's gun leaped into his hand and his finger pressed the trigger. The sixth bullet from the revolver of Peter Holcomb struck him in the breast and he joined his five riflemen upon the greensward. His bullet aimed at Pete, went wide, but it found a home, for it penetrated the right temple of Felix Dexter.

"Come on, Les!" shouted Holcomb, who was bounding toward the row of dead or wounded men. He picked up a fallen rifle, swung about like a flash and dropped one of Tabrano's men who had his gun at his shoulder. Gorman already had a rifle in his hand, but there was nobody to shoot. With shrieks of terror the natives had fled in all directions and with them went Tabrano's cohorts. The planter alone stood his ground and lifted his hands into the air as Pete covered him.

"Do you yield, *monsieur?*" Holcomb demanded.

"Of course," said Tabrano. "Am I not your friend, *senhor?*"

"That remains to be seen," replied Pete. "Cover him, Les, while I see to Louise."

For Louise, the stout-hearted, had fainted for the second time in her life; but this time it was from joy.

"Take care of her, *mon père,*" pleaded Pete to the priest as he lifted her tenderly in his arms. "There is a little cleaning up to be done here yet."

He ran to Tabrano and drew the revolver from his belt.

"Not that I distrust you, *senhor,*" he said with a grin, "but just as a matter of precaution."

Tabrano held out his hand.

"*Senhor* Holcomb," he exclaimed heartily, "never did I dream that such shooting was possible. Were it not for the bodies lying there I would not believe it now. When I gave you the weapon last night, it was out of pity for the young *senhorita* so that you might remove her from the terrible menace of Aguedarno."

"What's he talking about?" demanded Les who had come up and joined them.

"Tabrano lost his nerve last night and refused to do anything for us," explained Pete. "He couldn't, however, resist my offer to remove Aguedarno from his path before the firing-squad got me, and he agreed to leave my arms unbound so that I could plug Aguedarno when he gave the word to the firing squad."

"And you mowed down the whole outfit with six shots!" marveled Gorman. "Pete, I think you are the finest marksman in the world, and I come from the alleged wild and woolly West."

"THE FIRING squad was only twelve or fifteen paces distant. I could have hit six targets at that distance ninety-nine times out of a hundred, but the trick was to fire six shots before they could return one. I failed. Aguedarno got poor Felix."

"The man who feared death most was the one chosen to be killed," said Les sadly. "I was astonished that he was able to walk to execution."

"I bucked him up by telling him that they were blank cartridges," said Pete shamefacedly. "It was rotten, of course, but it kept him from going to pieces. If he had been in his senses he would have known that they would not have any blanks in the jungle. Tabrano, where is Sanchez confined?"

The balata man pointed to a hut back in the direction from which they had come to execution.

"See if Aguedarno is dead," commanded Pete, and Les did not hesitate to take his order.

"You hit him in the heart," he replied after he had rolled the body over and examined it. "Pete, such shooting is incredible. I don't believe you did it."

Pete grinned. "I never showed you my medals, did I? Tabrano, you listen to me. I have nothing against you; and Dexter, who owns this concession, is dead. I've removed your enemy Aguedarno and I'm going to leave you here in control because neither Mr. Gorman nor myself wishes to have anything more to do with balata."

"Oh, thank you, *monsieur!*"

"Only on condition that you obey orders. At the first sign of treachery I'll put a bullet through your heart. Order your men to bring in their arms and ammunition and deliver them to Mr. Gorman. Inform them that you die if one of them lifts a weapon against us. You keep alongside of him, Les, and plug him if he turns tricky. I'm going to see Louise."

Louise was standing with the *padre* a few rods away. She was still pale and weak, but she was again in control of herself and she was listening with glistening eyes to the priest's story of how Pete Holcomb, practically single-handed, drove off a tribe of savages who had attacked the mission.

"Well, Louise," Pete said softly, having come up behind her without her beings aware of it.

She whirled. "Pete, oh, Pete!" she cried tremulously and her arms went around his neck. In his exalted mood, this seemed the most natural thing in the world to Peter Holcomb who embraced her fiercely and rained burning kisses upon her willing lips.

"Oh, Peter, how wonderful you are! How grateful I am to you. How I love you," she murmured.

"That's all right, that's all right," he was muttering.

Louise suddenly stiffened and pushed him away from her.

"Oh, Peter!" she exclaimed, her cheeks crimson and hot. "What must you think of me? You don't love me. You don't even like me and I threw myself at you."

"Say," he cried indignantly. "How do you get that way? I've been crazy about you since the day you walked into the room when Les was hiring me as his secretary."

"You took a queer way of showing it," she demurred. "You never even told me I was pretty and you avoided me all the way down on the ship and right up to the day you disappeared."

"That was because—well, I promised Les not to make love to you, and I thought you had a case on Dexter."

"I didn't. Or if I did, I got over it. Where is Felix?"

"Felix? Didn't you see? Louise, the poor fellow was shot. He is dead."

Her eyes grew moist. "Everything was in a blur to me from the instant you began to shoot. Poor Felix! Oh, Pete, isn't everything terrible?"

"Everything was terrible until you let me kiss you," he replied. "Louise, we can't do anything about Felix. If you were carried away by excitement and didn't mean those kisses, it's all right."

"Don't you want me to mean them?" she asked wistfully.

"You can never know how I do! It means you—love me."

She smiled and held up her lips. He kissed her until she was breathless and then he heaved a deep, contented sigh.

"It's great to amount to something, at that," he declared.

FATHER PEDRO, who had stood within three feet during the passionate scene and whose existence they had completely forgotten, laid a hand on each head and began muttering a Latin blessing.

"Thank you, father," said Louise, blushing rosy red.

"My son," said the priest, "again you have taken human life, and to save your soul you must bitterly repent. However, if life must be taken I am glad that it was Dom Carlos who died. He was a very wicked man, perhaps the vilest in the world. It is unfortunate that he died without a chance to confess."

"I wouldn't hurt a fly, father," said Pete earnestly. "By nature I am the most peaceful person you can imagine: but I get put into the most terrible predicaments."

"I think you are a good man," said the priest gravely. "despite your deadly marksmanship; and I think that this is a good woman. Heaven bless you both."

"Louise," said Pete as he walked away, "that old fellow is a saint. Now, it isn't every day we are going to have the opportunity of being married by a saint."

"Oh, Pete, I couldn't," she protested. "Why, you've only just told me that you love me."

"It's something to think over," he urged. "Hello, Les. I'm going to marry your sister. Now what do you think of that?"

"I think Louise is getting a lucky break," replied Gorman, smiling broadly. "Pete, we've piled up all the guns and ammunition in our prison hut, and Tabrano didn't make the slightest attempt to double-cross us. What next—shall we let Sanchez out?"

"Yes, but tell him that he is still a prisoner. That bird has to be handled with gloves. Probably the only honest man in Brazil. I'll have to talk to him because you don't speak French. Take Louise up and put her to bed."

"I don't want to go to bed," protested Louise. "I want to stay with you."

Pete gave her his old-fashioned grin. "You do as you're told, young lady."

"All right," she said so meekly that Les stared at his sister with open mouth.

"You've got yours, good and plenty," he jeered.

She laughed joyously. "And how I love it," she proclaimed.

CHAPTER XXVIII

WHICH WAY TO TURN?

LATE THAT AFTERNOON there was a conference outside the former residence of Dom Carlos Aguedarno. The dead had been buried, the wounded were being cared for, and the natives were once more busily engaged in tapping balata trees and boiling and straining the gum.

Senhor Tabrano, after delivering up the arms of the settlement, had been allowed to go about his business. Pete was confident that the Brazilian was perfectly satisfied with the situation and would make no trouble.

The conversation between Pete, Louise, and Lieutenant Sanchez was in French, which Louise translated for the benefit of her brother. Sanchez had the floor.

"It is the regret of my life that I did not see your shooting, *monsieur,*" he declared. "Though, even if I had seen it with my own eyes, I could not tell the tale and be believed. You not only saved your own life and that of your companions, but you have also saved my own."

"Thanks for the compliment," grinned Pete jovially. "Glad to have been of service. Now let's get to our problem. Here we are a thousand miles from Manáos, only three of us, and the jungle full of Aguedarno's friends and our enemies. Old Parama is waiting to nab us if we go his way; my Indian friends may be waiting to gobble us up. We're in a fix."

"That is obvious."

"Well, you have an airplane. You can get us to Manáos in

two or three days. You profess to be grateful. All right. Take us along with you. Can you carry three persons besides yourself?"

Sanchez nodded "Unfortunately, I am in a predicament. I have warrants for your arrest, both of you, on a charge of murder. As soon as we enter the territory of Brazil, I am under obligations to apprehend you."

"But you don't call what I did here murder, I hope," said Pete tartly.

"Certainly not, *monsieur.* Aguedarno has influential friends in Manáos who will be eager to press these charges in revenge for his killing. I shall do what I can for you, of course, but I am only a naval lieutenant and I have no influence at all. The late Dom Juan da Sousa, if he were alive, might have come to your aid because of the affront Aguedarno put upon his daughter, which I would not fail to tell him."

"Wait a minute!" exclaimed Louise. "Les, old Sousa is dead. That means Rosa is free. She was engaged to Aguedarno and of course that's over now."

Les's eyes sparkled and his mouth worked with excitement. "Then we go to Manáos," he declared. "Rosa loves me, Louise. If the old man is dead, she will not hesitate to marry me in a minute."

Pete informed Sanchez of the situation and he looked sympathetic. "Senhorita da Sousa is the loveliest girl in Manáos," he stated, "and if she loves Senhor Gorman he is to be congratulated. Unfortunately, if you go to Manáos, you will be placed immediately under arrest, and despite your wealth, the situation of you and Monsieur Holcomb will be very serious."

"Then what the deuce can we do?" demanded Pete. "We can't go down to Manáos by the river and ever expect to get there, and we can't cross Colombia because Dexter, who knew the way, is dead. We certainly are not going to remain in this cursed place."

SANCHEZ reflected for a moment. "May I make a suggestion?" he asked.

"That's what I am hoping for."

"I am your prisoner. I must obey your orders. You have regained possession of your money and arms and supplies. If you point a gun at me and say, 'Sanchez, fly us in your seaplane to the nearest large city in Colombia,' I am forced to do as I am instructed." And he smiled eagerly.

"By Jove, that's it!" exclaimed Pete.

"You will have a long journey by bad trails from Mendico, but eventually you will reach Bogotá where you will be in civilization," continued the lieutenant. "The city of Mendico is between two and three hundred miles northwest of here, and there must be communication between it and the capital. Shall I take you there?"

"It's an order. Consider that a gun is pointed at your head," laughed Pete. "How will you manage about getting back?"

"It is possible that I can buy petrol at Mendico. If not, I must wait until a supply can be sent me from some other part of Colombia. I have no choice in the matter, being a prisoner." Sanchez chuckled.

"Will you ask the lieutenant if he will take a letter back to Manáos for me?" asked Gorman eagerly.

"To Rosa?" demanded Louise.

"Yes," he said defiantly. "Have you any objections?"

She shook her head. "Now that I know what it is to be in love, I withdraw all my objections. She is the most beautiful thing I ever saw and if she loves you, I hope you marry and are as happy as Pete and I are going to be."

"Thanks. Lou," Les Gorman said huskily.

"Speaking of marriage," remarked Holcomb, "I've had a talk with the *padre* and he can squeeze us in between his other engagements about eight o'clock to-morrow morning. In this wilderness the matter of a marriage license is overlooked and the *padre* won't ask questions about our religion. He is a primitive Christian and therefore broad-minded."

"Can't we wait, Pete, until we get back to New York or some other civilized place?" she asked meekly.

"Nope," he said firmly.

"Have I got to be married in trousers?" she wailed.

He chuckled. "I could get you one of these native women's costumes—a couple of yards of cotton cloth wrapped around the waist."

"Thanks, I prefer what I have on," she said hastily.

"Les," explained Pete, "I've seen this old priest under the most trying circumstances and he is the holiest man I have ever seen. If he marries us, I have a feeling that we'll be happy all our lives. How do you stand?"

Gorman smiled. "Can you support her in the manner to which she is accustomed?"

Pete scratched his head. "Well, in the manner to which she has recently been accustomed."

"Go to it, kids."

The resources of the settlement were taxed to provide a marriage feast that evening, for there would be no time for a wedding breakfast, since the takeoff would occur right after the ceremony in the morning.

Although the deaths of Scanlon and Dexter kept them from undue hilarity it was a very happy dinner. The good qualities of Felix were mentioned and his pitiful collapse overlooked, while the courage and loyalty of Scanlon were lauded to the skies.

Gorman had retrieved from Aguedarno's baggage the package of Brazilian bank notes taken from the supplies in the Gorman expedition's *montería*. After dinner he divided the pile in halves and presented one to the *padre* for the support of his mission.

The value of the cash reserves was fifty thousand dollars in American money and the munificence of the gift overcame the good father. Cash was useless in the jungle, of course, he explained, but with this money he could send it by Sanchez to buy materials to build a substantial church and construct a proper altar, and it would purchase in Manáos canned goods to be stored against a famine, and supply clothing for the converts. He recited a long prayer in Latin for the happiness of his benefactors.

THE CEREMONY, next morning, took place under the trees and was short, but impressive. The congregation included all the natives in the settlement and Tabrano's trusties. Les gave the bride away, Sanchez was best man and Louise was attended by two round-eyed Indian girls whose arms were filled with flowers.

A pretty touch was the idea of Tabrano who had sent his Indians into the jungle at dawn and who had strewn under the big tree where the marriage took place a carpet of orchids which would have been priceless in New York. Beautiful as they were, the lovely flowers had no value in that remote settlement.

Tabrano also supplied the wedding ring, for none of the Americans had worn an ornament into the jungle.

Sanchez, Les, and Gorman went through the ceremony with a rifle in their left hands for they were not lulled into security by the pretty attentions of the balata planter; but their precautions were unnecessary. As soon as Pete had kissed his bride, beautiful as a goddess despite her masculine costume, the party moved toward the river followed by several natives bearing the limited amount of supplies which the seaplane could carry, and accompanied by Tabrano and the *padre*.

As the priest knelt on the river bank and prayed for their safe conveyance they paddled out to the plane in a dugout and climbed on board. They were crowded somewhat, which did not irk Louise and Peter Holcomb, and they made themselves as comfortable as possible under the circumstances.

Sanchez started his engines, the propellers began to turn and were quickly making so much noise that they drowned out the shouts from the bank where the whole colony had suddenly appeared.

CHAPTER XXIX

CONCLUSION

IN A MOMENT they were in the air and Sanchez headed west-northwest. The lieutenant was as ignorant of the topography of that part of Colombia as his passengers, but from a height of three or four thousand feet he had a view of a hundred miles of country.

An hour passed and a hundred miles was traversed, but the land beneath was still an expanse of jungle, swamps, and little rivers; nor was there a sign of the smallest sort of settlement. Two hours went by and they were in higher country, with great stretches of meadows, occasional lakes and less dense forests. Ahead appeared a village and he headed toward it, but it was seen to be an Indian settlement and they did not descend.

In another half hour they sighted a small town with substantial houses and on the distant horizon a second settlement. Sanchez kept on to this and found it to be a white village of several hundred people, but he still refused to land. After another hour they spied what appeared to be a large town located upon a river, and they soared over it and inspected it from the sky.

The Brazilian nodded and began to descend. A couple of moments later they were resting on the breast of a small stream and grinning at the sensation the appearance of a plane had created in the village. There was a boat landing and a row of two and three-story houses facing the river. The bank was filling with white, brown, and black people among whom were several

men in the uniform of the Colombian army. As they gazed a
Ford came out of a side street and chugged to a stop at the head
of the quay. An army officer descended from it.

Sanchez looked back.

"My good friends, I think it is safe to leave you here. It
appears to be a military town, which means petrol for me and
some means of transportation for you. Are you satisfied?"

"We shall hate to say good-by to you." said Louise. "You have
been our salvation."

"As Monsieur Holcomb was mine," he replied. In Spanish
he shouted to the townsfolk to send out a boat to convey his
passengers ashore and immediately a large row-boat manned
by four men put out from the landing.

For the first time since their arrival in South America the
Americans felt that they were among friends. Later develop-
ments proved this to be true.

MENDICO proved to be a city of about a thousand inhabitants
of whom only about ten per cent were white. It was the station
of a company of soldiers and it possessed a hotel of a sort at
which the travelers were soon quartered.

As a Brazilian officer, Sanchez was immediately placed under
arrest for bringing a Brazilian government plane into Colombia without permission, and he was immediately released when
Gorman pressed a package of Brazilian bank notes into the
gratified hand of the commandant, who realized then that
Sanchez had come on an errand of mercy; and he invited them
all to be the guests of the Colombian army detachment situ-
ated in Mendico.

The quartet dined that night in the restaurant of the little
inn, through whose open and unscreened windows the population of the town stared in open-mouthed admiration.

Sanchez would be given petrol, at a price, and would start
for Manáos in the morning. The Americans would be conveyed
by Ford for some fifty miles, after which they must cross the
mountains on muleback to the plain of Bogotá. The journey

would be unpleasant and tedious, but their real perils lay behind them in the Amazon country. From Bogotá they would go by rail and plane to the coast where they would find a luxurious steamer to convey them to New York.

"After all," said Les Gorman, as they drank their coffee, "we had a perfectly glorious time, didn't we?"

Pete Holcomb set down his cup and stared at him in astonishment.

"Have you gone cuckoo?" he demanded.

"He means it, darling," said Louise. "He's that way."

"Boy-friend and classmate," replied Mr. Holcomb, "until yesterday morning I lived in misery and torture. I spent months in Hades. I don't even want to think of Brazil again."

Les laughed. "You've turned into a first-class he-man, Pete, and you can thank the Rio Negro for it. You were a weakling, a flop, a poor city sap. Now look at you."

"He was nothing of the kind!" said his wife angrily. "Pete was just as good a man as you ever were, with the addition of a perfectly lovely sense of humor."

"Oh, I admit that the stuff was there," said Les.

"And because a man messes around in wild places it doesn't follow that he is a finer person than one who lives comfortably in a city," she continued. "If it had been up to that big he-man Les Gorman, Pete would be in his grave and I would have been in the hands of that fiend Aguedarno."

"Darn it, I admit everything," exclaimed Les. "Pete is as good a man as I am with twice the brains. All I'm trying to show is that now he has learned what is really worth while in life and we three can go adventuring round the world—"

"Nix," stated Pete. "I'm going to get me a job in New York and never step off pavements again."

Louise laid a hand on his arm. "Wouldn't you even go to Paris, Pete, if I wanted to?"

"Oh, Paris. That's different. What I mean is that I crave civilized comforts."

"LOUISE won't be satisfied with that kind of life," the brother protested.

Louise laughed derisively. "Won't I, though! What Pete wants is what I want."

Gorman's face fell. "I was going to give you an interest in some big enterprise in some remote place, Pete, and the three of us would put it over."

"Louise is all I want from you, fellow," retorted Pete. "After you've gone broke trying to pull off big things in remote places you come to New York and Louise and I will give you a home. Won't we, baby?"

Louise smiled maliciously. "We can't have him living on us, though, darling. A big strong man like him!"

Les Gorman leaned back in his chair and surveyed the happy newlyweds contentedly.

"You make a good team," he stated. "I suppose you wouldn't consider, for a start, acting as New York representative of my Nevada interests at a salary of twenty thousand a year?"

"Certainly I wouldn't," replied Pete haughtily.

"Certainly you would!" snapped Louise. "Offer accepted, Les."

"*Madame,*" asked Sanchez in French, "it is not possible that our friends are quarreling?"

"Oh, no," she answered. "They are just two playful little gorillas. They are telling each other what they will do when they get back to North America, and they are not aware that they will do exactly what I decide is best for them."

"But of course," replied Sanchez with an understanding smile. "Will you ask Senhor Gorman if he will kindly write that letter to Senhorita da Sousa?"

Louise repeated the request.

"I'll write it immediately," he declared. "Lou, I'm going to send her funds and tell her that if she takes a steamer as soon as she receives my note she will be in New York about as soon as we will. Since you have run out on me, I'll try civilization for a while. But Rosa is the kind of girl who will be happy to do just what her husband wishes."

Louise laughed scornfully, "You lovesick elephant!" she retorted. "There are no such girls. Are there, Pete?"

He smiled fatuously. "None except you, darling."

Louise leaned over and kissed him. "You're going to find out a lot about me in the next forty or fifty years."

Pete rose, grinning. "That's as may be. Are you aware it's our wedding night?"

WHEN the fruit steamer which transported the explorers from Barranquilla to New York was halfway across the Gulf of Mexico, Les Gorman began to use the wireless. Pará reported that Senhorita Rosa da Sousa had sailed from that port on the steamer Pan-American three weeks before, and was due in New York four days ahead of their fruit boat.

Les's messages picked her up west of Cuba. For forty-eight hours he haunted the radio room, sending and receiving messages and aiding the wireless company to earn big dividends. Rosa was instructed to go to the Ritz, and to meet the steamer at the pier.

Les, armed with binoculars, picked her out in the crowd while the steamer was still half a mile from the dock. His gravity had dropped from him. He beamed like a boy and was watched with kindly amusement by the entire passenger list to whom the wireless courtship was no secret.

All eyes were on Rosa da Sousa when Les's shouts and her responses had identified her, and the general agreement was that she was the most beautiful brunette they had ever seen. Mrs. Peter Holcomb had already been voted the most beautiful blonde.

ABOUT THE AUTHOR

FRED MacISAAC IS so well known that *Argosy* readers will be surprised to learn that his first story was published as recently as November, 1924. It was a two-part serial entitled "Nothing but Money."

Previous to that time he had been a musical and dramatic critic upon New York and Boston newspapers, occupying an editorial chair after long years as a reporter and much knocking about the world. He brought to story writing a vast fund of personal experience and an enormous acquaintance among people of every walk in life. He was chummy with sea captains and grand opera singers, longshoremen and college professors, policemen and actors. He was a newspaper man in the days when the editorial room, not the counting room, was paramount. He made excursions into the field of press agenting. Once he traveled all over South America booking a tour for the Russian Ballet and transacted business in the Spanish tongue, which he learned during the sea trip between New York and Lima, Peru, and practiced upon the best people in Latin America.

As a concert manager and producer of open-air spectacles he was famous in New England. He once put on *Aida* in the open air, with two thousand people and a group of Metropolitan Opera stars in the cast, a ballet of a hundred, a stage band of fifty and an orchestra of one hundred, and twenty-five. He discovered a number of singers who have since climbed to the highest pinnacle of their art. While he was under the spell of music he followed opera all over the world, and heard it in Beirut, Milan, Paris, Vienna and Buenos Aires.

Fred MacIsaac

The film business is no mystery to him. He spent a year behind the scenes in the biggest studio in Hollywood, and says he prefers to write for magazines. He likes California and spends about half the year out where the palm trees rustle in the hot air provided by the Los Angeles boosters.

Many of his characters are lifted bodily out of life, which is the reason they seem so real to *Argosy* readers. Many of the incidents described in his stories are personal experiences. With all this background, he still considers himself a young man, and thinks the world is a very fine place.

Since fiction writing has emancipated him from the daily grind he roams all over the globe. Manuscripts drift in from Cairo, Central America or Hawaii, and every now and then he walks into the *Argosy* office and is annoyed to find the editor has an engagement for lunch.

THE ARGOSY LIBRARY ™

SERIES 1 INCLUDES:

* DENT * KETCHUM * KLINE *
* MacISAAC * ROSCOE *
* ROUSSEAU *
* SELTZER *
* TUTTLE *
* WIRT *
WORTS

THE BEST FICTION
FROM THE FRANK
A. MUNSEY LINE

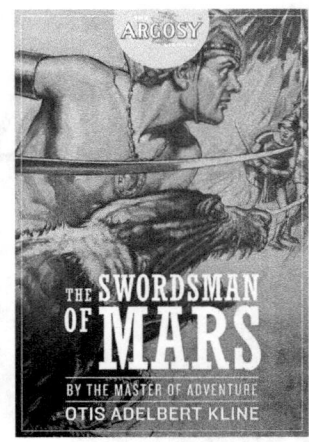

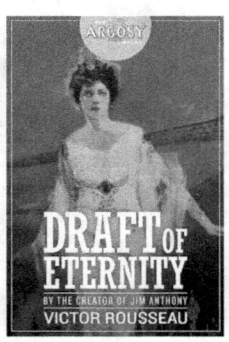